9.99

An Imperfect Librarian

An Imperfect Librarian

A NOVEL

ELIZABETH MURPHY

BREAKWATER BOOKS LTD.

JESPERSON PUBLISHING • BREAKWATER DISTRIBUTORS

100 Water Street • P.O. Box 2188 • St. John's • NL • A1C 6E6
www.breakwaterbooks.com   www.jespersonpublishing.ca

Library and Archives Canada Cataloguing in Publication

Murphy, Elizabeth, 1958-
    An imperfect librarian / Elizabeth Murphy.

ISBN 978-1-55081-247-3

I. Title.

PS8626.U753I46 2008   C813'.6   C2008-903100-8

The Canada Council | Le Conseil des Arts
for the Arts | du Canada

We acknowledge the financial support of The Canada
Council for the Arts for our publishing activities.

We acknowledge the support of the Department of Tourism,
Culture and Recreation for our publishing activities.

Canada

We acknowledge the financial support of the Government of
Canada through the Book Publishing Industry Development
Program (BPIDP) for our
publishing activities.

Printed in Canada.

Mixed Sources
Product group from well-managed
forests, controlled sources and
recycled wood or fiber
FSC   www.fsc.org Cert no. SW-COC-000952
© 1996 Forest Stewardship Council

MAN, THE IMPERFECT LIBRARIAN
MAY BE THE PRODUCT OF CHANCE
OR OF MALEVOLENT DEMIURGI.

— JORGES LUIS BORGES

for

JIMMY & MAISIE

the bibli-oasis

I MET HENRY DURING MY first week of work at the library. Of all the people they could have picked to orient me, they chose him. The orientation, if I can call it that, turned out to be nothing more than an afternoon at the campus cafeteria listening to his rant about how the Internet was going to corrupt the soul of the library, diminish our collective intelligence and turn books into relics. I'd heard it all before.

"You can't stop the flood with a finger poked in the dyke," I said. "One of these days, it's going to explode. If you're not prepared, you'll be washed away."

Henry shook his head then eyed me as if to say I should know better. "If there's any poking in a hole, it won't be with my finger." That was it for the conversation and I've been avoiding talk of floods and fingers ever since.

The orientation ended with a summary. "The most important fact you need to know about this library is that Information Services Librarian Henry Kelly takes a break every afternoon at 3:30. We'll meet at the cafeteria tomorrow to continue. I don't mind sacrificing my spare time for a good cause. If you have any questions, you can ask me then. I'll be sure to know the answer."

I saw Henry that next day, the next and the next, 3:30, at the campus cafeteria. The location and time never varied. Nor did his complaints. "How much for a medium stale coffee plus two of those shrivelled-up biscuits?" he said to the girl.

Later, while he scouted for a table, I cleaned up after him. "He's the same with me," I whispered to her. "Don't take it personally."

It wasn't long after that I proposed we have our coffee breaks in my office. He'd provide the coffee and cookies. I'd supply the coffeemaker and location. At the time, I assumed it was a fair bargain. The alternative would have been his basement office in the Librarians' Auxiliary Branch, but Henry had already rejected that idea. "I wouldn't have my coffee break in the LAB if Tim Horton showed up in person to serve me. No walls, no windows, no peace or quiet, no respite from the persistent drone of mindless chatter. You can't even pick your nose in private." He raised a finger, shook it at me and said, "Consider yourself lucky to have this office."

My office is one of those if-you've-seen-one-you've-seen-them-all kinds of spaces: metal filing cabinet, bookcase, desk and chair, two monitors, keyboard, mouse, electronic stylus, picture of my wife Elsa, two chairs facing the window, one for Henry, one for me, and finally, a makeshift coffee stand that I clean after his messy visits. The whole lot is sandwiched between fluorescent ceiling lights and wall-to-wall, grey industrial carpet that doesn't hide the stains. Opposite the door is the view down into the Special Collections Reading Room of King Edward University Library.

The best part about the office is that view. Henry can describe it better than me. I've heard him call it sublime – as in the LAB's the ridiculous, the Room's the sublime or a house of worship: "What's happening in the house of worship today, Carl?" It's not only the architecture that he raves about. "The rest of this library is a desert – a wasteland of floor after floor, stack after stack, book after book, page after page, word after word, letter after letter of volumes that have never been borrowed, never been read or noticed. You're looking straight down onto an oasis with some of the rarest, most precious manuscripts and volumes in the country."

When Henry comes by in the mid afternoon, he eyes the happenings in the Room so intensely you'd swear he'd forked out a fortune on a scalped ticket for the privilege. Occasionally, he'll overstay his welcome and I have to ration the cookies to get him to leave. He stuffs them into his mouth with assembly-line precision using his right hand then washes them down with coffee using his left. He doesn't hesitate to make himself at home. "How's the spectacle today, Carl? Any new developments? Move your chair. Stop hogging the view."

I never was much of a Winnie-the-Pooh reader as a child, but I remember the image of the short, stocky, wobbly bear with the shrunken red shirt only half covering his belly. Henry reminds me of him, especially when he wears that red polo shirt he's surely had in his wardrobe for the last century. It passes for respectable from the chest up. The problem is around the waist. Between the top of his trousers and the bottom of his shirt is a too-generous view of a hairy stomach with a navel as round and deep as an artesian well.

I don't visit his office often, but I've seen the photo of his three grown sons on his desk. They're posed in descending order of height with Henry on the low end. All four have their arms crossed and are wearing matching red and black sweaters. The photo reminds me of a set of those wooden Russian dolls, more broad than tall, that nest inside each other. Henry would know what they're called.

I joked with him once that people might assume he was pregnant with twins if he didn't cover up with a longer shirt.

"The Irish famine ended more than a hundred years ago," he said. "Where've you been?" He sized me up toe to crown. "There's more meat on Good Friday. Bugger off or I might give birth to the twins on your grimy office floor."

Henry has a stash of parting lines stored I-don't-know-where. He drops one whenever he exits my office, like an actor walking off stage to thundering applause. That time, I could only make out the words "giant with a dwarf's prick."

I'd heard variations on that line in the schoolyard when I was a boy. Comments about my height don't bother me anymore, especially not from Henry. He'd be starved without an audience and I crave the diversion.

CHAPTER TWO

the abridged version

THE LAST TIME WE VISITED the campus cafeteria together was October 1999, one month after I moved to Newfoundland. We were scouting for a place to sit when we noticed some people from the library. One of them happened to be a young, pretty woman, fresh from graduate school.

"She's been giving me the eye," Henry said as we walked towards her. "She's after me for sure. And why shouldn't she be?" He sauntered up to the table; you'd think he was James Bond. His cough was like a knock on a door. No one answered. We sat down anyway. He took the free chair by her side. I found a place across from him.

The man next to me introduced himself. "You're new here at the library, aren't you?"

I nodded.

"You'll be fine in no time," he said, and turned back to the conversation. I noticed Henry sitting tall on the edge of his chair, hands in his lap, eyes glued to the face of the woman. A minute later, I glanced at him again and he was still staring. I tried to kick at him under the table. I missed. The woman jerked upward in her chair then turned to face Henry.

"Will you come to a movie with me this Saturday?" he said without introduction or warning.

"Are you serious?"

"Dead," he replied.

She slid her chair away from the table and slung her purse over her shoulder as she stood up. "Pick on someone your own size," she said without a glance at him. He didn't take his eyes off her until she'd disappeared into the crowd.

As if the incident hadn't even occurred, Henry turned to face the conversation around the table. Someone was reminiscing about Christmas in the outports during the twenties and thirties. "If you found an orange under the tree, you were grateful. We didn't get spoiled back in them days," the person said.

Up until that moment, I didn't think Henry was really paying attention. Then, out of nowhere, he said, "You think you had it bad? Sure, where I lived in Ireland, if you didn't wake up Christmas morning with a hard-on, you had nothing to play with."

I was the only person who laughed. One by one, they rose from the table and pushed in their chairs. They dropped words behind them like crumbs: *vulgar, infantile, rude, juvenile, pig.* Henry heard them too, although he acted as if he hadn't. He smiled and drank his coffee with a my-it's-a-grand-day air about him. Not long after they'd gone, he looked at me with a halo of feigned wonder. "I was only telling the truth," he said.

"I can't believe you would actually talk about hard-ons like that with those people."

"Go on with ya, ya sissy."

"The *pick on someone your own size* was a bit much."

"She doesn't know what she's missing," Henry said. "As

Chesterton wisely observed, better to have loved a short man than not at all." He washed the comment down with a mouthful of coffee.

I don't have any experience with being short. I've always been in the ninetieth percentile for height. That means only ten percent of the population looks as out of place in a crowd as I do. It also means that, as a child, I was easy prey for school bullies. The earliest incident I can remember was during the first week of school. I believed them when they said that, if the bathroom door at the back of class was closed, someone was in there. The teacher was doing a lesson. "There are rivers, ponds, lakes, oceans, seas, streams," she said. "Do we drink the water from the ocean or…"

I glanced over my shoulder while she talked about what we do when we're thirsty. The bathroom door was closed. Much later, while we practiced our printing with words like *gush, flow, dribble, drop* and *flood*, it was still closed. Later that day, I tried to explain all that to Papa. He didn't say anything except that, if it happened again, he'd make me sit in my wet pants until I went to bed.

"Will we have another apple flip and coffee or will we go back now to the library?" Henry said.

"It's already four and we'll be going home at six o'clock. It's two hours before supper and only three hours after lunch. If you consider lunch from the time it ends at two o'clock then that's only two hours ago. If you–"

"You're a sissy with a math problem," he said. "Give me the abridged version next time."

That evening, after work, Henry offered me a ride home. Along the way, we stopped at the supermarket. We were heading towards his car in the pelting rain when we spotted a frail old woman, hunched over with her plastic grocery bags in either hand. She was about to step off the curb into a deep puddle between two parked cars. Henry hurried over to her, carrying his own bags. "Wait here!" he called above the howl of the wind. He grabbed her groceries, stepped into water up to his calves, waded to the taxi, then opened the door. A blast of loud rock music shot out from inside. He laid the bags on the floor, ordered the driver to move ahead, then closed the door. He splashed back through the puddle to the woman and led her along a dryer route.

After they drove off, I asked Henry where his bags were. We realized then what had happened to them. "All the better," he said. "She'll be delighted with the bargain. They don't call it SaveEasy for no reason."

Henry and I never went back to the cafeteria for coffee after that day. From then on, we met at 3:30 in my office. I doubt anyone missed us.

CHAPTER THREE

a portrait of the librarian as a young man

APPARENTLY, I DON'T LOOK LIKE a Newfoundlander. Same reaction when I tell people my father's French and my mother Spanish. "You're too tall to be a Latin type," they say. Sometimes, I'll respond with, "It was a vintage year." They usually don't get it. I don't resemble a librarian either. "You're joking." I've heard that response often enough when I tell people what I do for a living. One of these days, I'll experiment, grow a bun, borrow a pair of round-rimmed spectacles, a turtleneck, put a finger like an oboe reed to my lips for *shush*, wear a long skirt instead of a tie and see what happens. Not even my colleague Edith is that stereotypical, and if anyone looks like a librarian, it's her.

I told Papa I was planning to do a master's degree in library science after I finished my undergraduate degree in computer science. "Nonsense," he said. "There's no science to checking in and out books. It's a woman's profession, always was, forever will be."

It was worse when I told him what kind of librarian. He said he didn't raise me to be a technician. I wanted to say: You didn't raise me, period. Instead, I said: It's a science not a technique. He said: Don't hide behind fancy titles, and I wanted to say: Can't you pat me on the back for once? But I said: Digital Library Systems is the exact title, and he replied: Worse still.

I worked in a library shelving books throughout much of my first degree. Sometimes I miss those years. Mostly I miss the BC. There's no other library like it anywhere. It's where I used to spend my spare time. I had a surplus of it in those days. There was a group of us students working at the public library near campus. We used to play a game to see who could navigate the circulation system the fastest. Losers had to shelve a portion of the winner's books. It didn't take me long to master the system. If I saw the number 636.7, I knew the book was about dogs. A few details and I could rhyme off the catalogue number to the decimal. I won the game every time.

While someone else was shelving my books, I went to the basement stacks where they sent the overflow, oversized, underused, and damaged volumes. I spent every minute experimenting with different cataloguing systems – tall books over there, small here, books I fancy on those shelves, ones I'm not interested in on these and so on. After a while, everyone started calling it Brunet's Closet or the BC for short. I'd hear them say: "New shipment for the BC," or "Send the volumes to the BC."

I've had a relationship with libraries since I was little. When I was in the elementary grades, Papa had appointments on Tuesdays and Thursdays. On those afternoons, I stayed in the library when classes ended. I sat in the same chair each time. It was big enough for me to lie down on if I curled my legs. One afternoon, I read a storybook about a boy who rushes home from school every day to play with his best

An Imperfect Librarian

friend Marcel. Marcel is a mutt. No cat, no bone, no fire hydrant ever gets his attention more than the boy. Likewise, the boy feeds him before he feeds himself. He rubs Marcel's belly so much the creature spends more time on his back than on his paws. The boy comes home early from school one afternoon when everyone is anxious to be sheltered from the rain and wind that's causing the river to flood, trees to fall and walls of old barns to cave in. The dog doesn't run to the door and bark the way he normally would. "Marcel," the boy calls. He waits for him to appear from under a bed or from the bathroom where the dog sometimes steals a fresh drink out of the toilet. "Marcel." He hollers, this time an order: "Marcel!"

Even a boy can be patient when it concerns a dog. He understands Marcel. He knows his friend can't help chasing after a cat or wandering off with another dog who's come visiting from the farm. It's when he goes to bed that the boy really misses him. He gets through the night because he knows he's going to find him the next day. In the morning, he cleans and shines the dog's bowl before he fills it with fresh water. He sprinkles some cheese on top of the dog food, the kind Marcel likes best. He rides his bike past the school all the way to the creek where they go swimming together on lazy summer afternoons. Later, he visits the town's main road where he sometimes brings Marcel on a leash, proud to show off the smartest dog in town.

He goes to bed again, this time convinced that Marcel will appear the next day. He knows he'll want to scold him for misbehaving, but he'll hug and scratch him behind the ears and Marcel won't run away anymore. In the morning, he opens a fresh tin of food then fills the bowl with an extra helping because Marcel will be hungry when he returns.

Then, one night when it's so cold the bedroom radiator is making popping noises, the boy reaches over to cuddle into the dog. The cold, empty space that should be warm tells him what he doesn't want to know. If Marcel were there, he'd lick the boy's salty face and the pillow wouldn't be wet in the morning. The boy doesn't fill the dog's bowl that day. On his way to school, he decides that he'll never own another dog.

I never had a dog. I didn't even have any friends with one. But I felt better for the boy after I hid that storybook behind a shelf in the school's library so no one else would read it. I'm certain it was after that incident that I decided I wanted to be a librarian.

CHAPTER FOUR

cyclops and binoculars

H ENRY STANDS UP TOO FAST and triggers the nerve problem in his back. He winces, then limps over to the coffee stand in the corner of my office. He's wearing his red shirt with the built-in air-conditioning around the waist. He pours another cup, wobbles past my desk, then settles into his chair. He inhales the steam and sighs. "Imagine a library within a library, collections within collections," he says. "Imagine centuries of maritime documents, correspondence, logs, journals, maps, letters, diaries. You should consider it a privilege to own an office overlooking the Reading Room, Carl. If it were mine, I'd do nothing but gaze down there all day long."

"Some of us have work to do."

"And others have more important things to do than work. Open your eyes, man! Look!" He jabs his arm upward like he's stabbing the air with a sword.

"It's the same every day."

"That's where you're wrong. Always on Wednesday and Friday, always at 3:45, always in the same reading carrel, bag by her left side every time. Watch her more closely. She just put something in her bag. She's up to something for sure." Henry wipes his lips with his hands then pokes my shoulder like he's trying to tip me over. "I said she's up to something for sure. Are you listening, Carl?"

"More or less. I was half thinking about something else."

"There's not much point in your company if there's only half of you in attendance. Not to mention your famine version of biscuits and coffee. I might as well go to the cafeteria. Watch. See how she slid something into the bag?"

"Maybe."

"What you need is a pair of binoculars."

My binoculars were a goodbye gift from friends who'd heard Newfoundland was an ideal location for spotting rare birds. "Look for the white tufts on their heads," they told me.

I go home later that day and dig them out of a suitcase I haven't got round to unpacking yet. They're wrapped in a multi-coloured summer shirt that's too tropical for the Newfoundland climate. I bring them to the office the next morning where the plan is we'll take turns. We shut off the lights so we can't be noticed by anyone in the Room.

"That's enough, Henry. You're not even watching her. If anyone ever caught you, they'd hang you. Pass them to me."

He pushes the binoculars into my hands without looking my way. He rises out of his chair, grabs his crotch then shakes it as if someone had dropped something into his trousers that he wants to dislodge. I lean forward in my chair and play with the focus.

"If I didn't know better, I'd think I was gazing into a Gothic cathedral."

"It's Edwardian, not Gothic," says Henry.

"Whatever. Why is the Room antique when the rest of the library is modern? Is it older?"

"It's Edwardian, not antique or Gothic. It's younger not

older. The Reading Room was added onto this side of the building ten years after the library first opened. Your office window once overlooked blinding sunlight on snow in April and capelin weather in June. The benefactor dictated the style: stained-glass windows, vaulted ceiling, hardwood floors, fake Persian rugs around the couches and chairs. All that's missing is the fireplace, chandeliers and marble staircase. It's not the Rose Reading Room in the New York Public Library, but it has grandeur and sophistication."

I scan along the walls, straight ahead, slowly. "I expect a pigeon to come flying off one of the arches."

"They're columns in the Ionic order, not arches," he says. "Edwardian, remember. Not Gothic. You should outfit yourself with the equivalent of binoculars for your ears."

"The binoculars are designed for bird-watching. They're too hard to focus indoors."

"If that's the case, give them to me," he says as he tugs on my arm. I ignore him and stand next to the window. I search for her carrel then focus in and out again. Something blocks my view. I adjust the focus, step closer to the window and feed Henry the play by play. "Looks like a baby's bum, pink and shiny."

"Sounds like Francis," Henry says.

"It's him all right. He's bending down to whisper in her ear. Do you think he coats that bald scalp in makeup?"

"If Francis Hickey, mighty Head of Special Collections, went outside on a clear day, his head would be visible in remote galaxies. He's pedicured, manicured, UV-rays cured. You should see him jogging down Water Street in his black spandex suit. A few years ago, he tried to pass a motion at Library Council to introduce a dress code. He said we can't expect patrons' respect if we're dressed like bums and smell no better. You can imagine who he was staring at while he said it. You won't catch me wearing spandex. If I had his face, I'd wear it inside out."

CYCLOPS AND BINOCULARS

I step forward for a closer view. She's sitting with her back facing me on the other side of the Room under one of the stained-glass windows. Francis is leaning over her with his arm on her shoulder. His black turtleneck sweater and naked head block my view again. He turns, and before I realize what's happened, he's staring straight at me.

"*Merde!*" In a panic, I make one of those impulsive jerks backward like I'm reeling from a dangerous object. In the process, I bang into Henry's chair, trip, then hit his arm before I fall.

"Jesus! My shirt. Look at the mess of coffee on there now. You don't understand, Carl, the binoculars only make objects *seem* closer."

His hairy navel is staring at me like a Cyclops. I drag myself up off my office floor, binoculars in one hand, holding onto my desk with the other. I look down into the Room. "I bet Francis is en route to my office right this second. I knew I shouldn't have bothered with the binoculars."

"You shouldn't have indeed," says Henry.

"The binoculars were your idea. What are you talking about?"

"Who cares about binoculars? Stand up to the prick!" On the word *prick*, crumbs shoot out of his mouth. He brushes them off one leg of his trousers and splatters coffee over the other.

A number of people, Henry included, are opposed to the library's strategic emphasis on computers. I can't blame them. If there's one role that the Internet is going to change, it's the librarian's. You don't need to be Nostradamus to predict that. Who needs a librarian if all the knowledge in the world is at your fingertips? I'm not surprised that the other librarians are wary of what I do. They didn't support spending a chunk of the budget on a new digital systems unit. But they don't take it out on me personally. *They* don't. Francis does. One of the first moves I made when I began my position was to get access to all administrative databases on campus. I can't be expected to do my job efficiently without it.

I wanted to explain that to Francis so I asked for a meeting with him. He invited me to his office. I went straight to my purpose. I told him I'd set up access to all the databases; I'd visited the different units and understood how they operated. Next, I described my vision to digitize Special Collections materials in five to ten years. I explained that I'd need access to his databases, inventories of materials, information about how materials were presently organized and catalogued, plans for future acquisitions and so on.

He listened carefully and didn't interrupt or ask any questions, even when I explained some of the more complex details about how the access would be centrally controlled by software designed especially for the library. I finished what I had to say then waited for his reaction. He was leaning so far back in his chair, I was afraid he'd tip over. He brushed something off his shoe. When I asked him how that sounded to him, he told me it sounded like I was telling him how to run his unit. I explained that wasn't what I meant. This was a great opportunity for collaboration, I told him.

"You mind your affairs and I'll mind mine. How's that for collaboration?" he said then rose out of his seat, opened his office door and motioned for me to leave.

If I had my time back now I probably wouldn't have complained to the Chief Librarian. I would have waited a few days instead of firing off the letter that very instant when I was frustrated and angry. I shouldn't have cc'd Francis on it. The Chief called the two of us in for a meeting. Francis said he'd be more than willing to work with me. Not a problem. Of course I could have access to his databases and inventories, whatever and whenever I needed. "Come for a tour anytime," he said.

I left the meeting after the three of us had shaken hands. As a rule, I take the stairs, not the lift. I have to remind myself to substitute elevator for lift, cellphone for mobile, truck for lorry, apartment for flat and so on. The stairs are adjacent to my office, whereas the elevator is at the other end of the corridor by Edith's office. I don't want to encourage her by walking past. She doesn't need an excuse to think I might be interested in her. The stairwell door closed shut behind me. I trudged up the dirty concrete steps. I'd almost made it to the main landing and was thinking this was another occasion where I'd completely misread the situation. I'd fussed about Francis for nothing. The door opened and closed below. Someone was rushing up the steps behind me. I stopped to let them pass while I caught my breath. It was Francis.

"I forgot to mention a few items at our meeting," he said, standing on the steps next to me. "Don't think you're going to play with my databases, inventories, future acquisitions anymore than you're going to play with my dick. The sooner you get that straight, the sooner we'll be able to tolerate each other. In the meantime, throw sand in my face again like you did with that letter to the Chief and I'll bury you in concrete."

That was my last face-to-face conversation with Francis. I've been avoiding him ever since.

I don't want to open my office door if it means having to explain what I was doing with the binoculars, but the knock is persistent. "Hello," the voice on the other side calls. The pitch is too high to be Francis. I open. She's leaning against the wall, arms folded, frowning. "I knew you were here. I saw you come in after lunch. Oh, I see. Henry's here with you."

"Edith, come on in," Henry says. "I'm sure Carl would be delighted to welcome you. He was remarking recently how much he enjoys your company. See you two lovebirds later."

"Sorry, Edith. Henry's teasing again."

"No need to apologize. I'll be your lovebird any day."

Henry winks at me then goes out the door, leaving me to clean up after him in more ways than one.

hola mamá

I COULD HAVE GONE BACK TO the Chief to tell him what Francis said on the stairwell. But it's reporting that upset Francis in the first place. I should have known that would happen. The last time I reported on someone it backfired as well. It was only a couple of years after Papa and I moved to France from Quebec. There were three boys in particular who were causing me problems. What they lacked in centimetres they made up for in brazenness. Sometimes I thought their only pastime was playing tricks on me. I'd come home from school with my clothes torn, my face, arms or legs scratched and bruised. Papa would say, "You're taller than boys twice your age. Fight back!" My height didn't work as a weapon. On the contrary – that, plus the remains of my Québécois accent, made me an easy target for their pranks. It didn't help that they knew I was a bastard child. They'd figured that much out – heard it from their parents probably.

They used similar ploys each time. "She wants to touch your dicky," they said once. I was on my way home in my new outfit. Papa had bought it for the beginning of the school year. "Don't let me find a spot on it," he warned me. He didn't need to worry. I was so proud of my long pants, new vest and shirt, I wouldn't even allow dust to touch them. The bowtie was uncomfortable but I was afraid I'd lose it if I took it off. I was the finest dressed of anyone that day. I thought that's why the boys seemed to be behaving differently towards me.

"She's in the park," they said as they led me there. "Wait on the bench. We'll get her for you."

I leaned back on the bright green bench and waited. At the time, I used to believe things happened faster if you closed your eyes. The time did go fast with my eyes closed, but I couldn't wait forever because Papa would be upset if I came home late. Eventually I left. Not long after, I met up with the boys again. "She didn't come," I told them. They said nothing. They were too busy laughing to talk.

Papa was there when I arrived. He was at home every afternoon because he didn't have a job yet. "Where were you?" he said.

"In the park."

"Go take off your good clothes before you sit at the table to do your homework."

I headed to my room. I couldn't wait to take off the bowtie.

"Carl!" he roared. As soon as I saw the expression on his face, I knew what I was in for. I did what he said. I stripped down to my skin. My clothes lay in a pile on the floor with the horizontal stripes of green paint facing upwards. Papa felt better after giving me a spanking. I felt better knowing he felt better.

It didn't end there, although I wished it could have. He packed the soiled clothes in a bag and we went to see the principal the next day. The principal gave me an apple to chew on while Papa shouted at him. When Papa left, I went to my classroom with the principal. He carried the bag and held my hand. He didn't grip it tightly the way Papa usually did. The three boys were in the back row. I stood by the principal's side and ate my apple.

He pulled my clothes out of the bag. "Who is responsible? Who?" He knew who they were, but he asked anyway. He held my trousers, shirt and vest in front of him, shaking them. We weren't used to him shouting. No one said anything. He turned to face me. I thought he was going to order me to stop eating the apple.

"What did the boys do to you, Carl? Tell everyone," he said.

"They told me to sit on the bench, sir."

"Why did they tell you to sit on the bench?"

"To wait for the girl, sir."

"What girl?"

"The girl I was waiting for, sir."

"Why were you waiting for the girl?"

"Because they told me to, sir."

"Yes, but *why* did they tell you? Why did you need to wait for the girl?"

"Because they tol–"

"I know they told you, Carl," he said. He shook his head and smiled at the class. They seemed more relaxed after that. In the row on the side, Marianne let out a giggle then cupped her hand over her mouth to hide it.

"Tell me why you wanted to wait for the girl, but don't say it was because the boys told you to do it."

"No, sir. I won't say the boys told me to do it, sir."

He turned to face the class once again, shaking his head. The boys who'd made me do it shook their heads too.

"Tell me why!"

"Because you told me not to, sir."

I put the half-eaten apple in the pocket of my jacket and

looked up at him. He seemed to be trying not to laugh.

"One last time. Tell me why you wanted to wait for the girl. Was she going to bring you candy, a book, a message? Why did you sit on the bench to wait for the girl?" At that point, I'd almost forgot the conversation had anything to do with the bench.

"Because the boys–"

He let out a small chuckle. That was all the audience of six-year-olds needed. They broke out in laughter like a sudden applause at the end of a great performance. Even Marco was laughing and I don't think I'd ever seen him laugh before. I laughed because I thought I should do what they were doing. That made it funnier for them, but I'd rather be laughed at than stand in front of the class and admit I was waiting for a girl to touch my dicky.

Not long after the incident, Papa decided it would be best for me to live with his twin sister Georgette. Tatie or Auntie is what I called her. When she followed her husband Philip to England not long after my ninth birthday, she took me with her. I couldn't live with my mother because there was no mother beyond the one-night stand between Papa and another graduate student. They met at a party a few months after he arrived in Quebec to go to university. They got drunk, had sex and he never saw her again. Nine months later, she called him from the hospital to ask if he wanted to take the baby.

Her Catholic family in Spain would have disowned her if they knew. There were English-speaking, Protestant families in Montréal who would have taken me, but in 1950, no respectable French-speaking Catholic family would have anything to do with an illegitimate child. Papa didn't care that the potential adopters were Protestant. And he didn't mind the Irish. "We go way back," he said. But he'd never in a million years allow his lineage to fall to anyone with Anglo-Saxon ties.

An Imperfect Librarian

When I turned eighteen, Papa gave me her name. That was all he could remember. Then the web came along. Suddenly, the world was so much smaller. I typed her name into a search engine. Within a few clicks, she appeared on the screen. She's a retired anthropology professor at the University of Barcelona. Her photo is on their web site. For a while, I used it for my computer background so I could see her picture every day.

I sent her emails. I thought she might want to know that her son bears a striking resemblance to her: pitch-black hair, dark eyes, olive-coloured skin. I tried a creative selection of subject lines. There was the variation on the *Hola mamá* plus *Baby from Quebec hospital* as well as *Remember Georges Brunet? I'm his son* and, towards the end when I was frustrated and said things I later regretted, *You're being selfish & cruel to your son.* The caption on the photo read: *Professor Margarita Xavier-Manzares, her husband Dom Fernandez, their daughters Gabriella and Maria and their only son Manuel.*

i count, therefore, i am

ENRY'S *STAND UP TO THE prick* reminds me of Papa's *Fight back*. I'll stand up to the prick on the day Henry resolves to learn to use the computer. That's not going to be anytime soon. The attendance lists come back to me after training sessions. Never do I see the name *Henry Kelly*. At Department Head meetings, if his name is mentioned, I make excuses for him: "He probably didn't know about the session. I'll work harder on publicising them." Another time, I said I was training him privately. It's a good thing Henry didn't hear that.

He comes for coffee one afternoon when there's a session on online information search tactics that he's supposed to be participating in.

"How come you're not at training today?" I ask him.

"I won't be wasting my valuable intelligence on a passing fad. I'll leave the staring at a screen to illiterate philistines like yourself." He pours a coffee, raises the cup to his lips, takes a mouthful, then spits it out.

"Would you do that on the floor of your own office?" I ask

An Imperfect Librarian

him. "I bet you wouldn't."

He unfolds a strip of paper towel from the stand, drops it on the coffee stain, then stamps on it. "Jesus. Who drinks day-old coffee?"

"I do."

"Maybe that's what's wrong with you."

He takes the pot to the hallway to rinse it in the water fountain. When he returns, he brushes me out of the way disdainfully with the type of hand that shoos birds. Next, he sniffs the grounds with the attention of a perfume designer. He pours the water with the calculated science of a chemist. Finally, he presses the switch like he's restoring power to a city after a blackout. When that's done, he folds his arms and eyes the pot as if it couldn't perform except under his supervision. "It's time for you to stand up to Francis," he says. "He thinks he has a prick so long he can fuck everyone who comes near him."

"Why don't you do it?"

"I've been around here too long. It takes someone new, someone like yourself from the outside," Henry says.

"Francis has a committee, a campaign, a draft of a privacy policy, promotional materials. How can I compete?"

"Find yourself a Stephen Blumberg."

"Never heard of him."

"I could pretend he's the top striker for Manchester United," he says. "You wouldn't know the difference, would you?"

"I never was much of football fan. I'd favour Arsenal over Manchester United, if I was."

"Blumberg is to book theft what Bruce Reynolds is to train robbery. A mastermind."

"He can't be that brilliant if he was caught."

Henry crosses his arms and rests them on top of his belly. He spreads his legs to balance his weight. "They nabbed

Blumberg after he'd stolen twenty thousand rare books plus ten thousand manuscripts from hundreds of libraries in Canada as well as the States. He's the greatest American book thief of the twentieth century."

He pours his coffee. I pour mine. We take our seats as if the show's set to begin.

"That's sixty or seventy books a day for a year."

"Add to that all the time he spent scheming," says Henry.

"He'd need a shopping cart for that many volumes."

"His techniques were more subtle: everything from false IDs to stolen keys. My personal favourite is the simplest." Henry brushes off his fingers on the armrest of his chair then raises one finger at a time for each item. "Locate the books, check them out, bring them home, remove the protective magnetic strip, return them to the library the following day." Next, he holds up the other hand. "Return to the library, remove the books from the shelf, conceal them under your clothes, stroll out of the building." For the finale, he turns his outstretched hands palms up. "No magnetic strip, no alarm."

"Clever scheme for sure. Not foolproof though."

Henry crosses his legs and leans back in his chair. "Not quite. One of the libraries maintained a digital archive of borrowers' records. They knew exactly who'd borrowed what, when. They were missing a particular book, checked their records and voilà. Since I'm not in the habit of boring people with detail, the rest you can imagine. Find yourself a miniature Blumberg. Prove that tracking patrons' borrowing histories can catch thieves and you'll have them eating out of your computer. Speaking of eating." He goes to the coffee stand while I stare ahead into the Room.

Henry's not the only one who doesn't understand my project. It's meant to make best use of information on borrowing and querying. What types of books are borrowed the most, longest or never? At what time of day, week or year are the most books borrowed? Do faculty or males query the database more than students or females? What are they searching for? I was relieved when the Chief Librarian asked me to give a talk at Library Council to explain the project. The timing was ideal. The Internet had just taken off. It was a historic moment in the evolution of libraries. I was there to be a catalyst for great change. I thought maybe some day people would look back on the work I did as a great achievement. I dreamed of getting an award.

I arrived to give my talk. The Chief introduced me. I was about to speak when a hand went up. It was a comment for the Chief from Francis. "Before any more money is spent on digital systems, a committee needs to be created to set a strategy and goals for what we want this library to look like in five or ten years time…" When he finished talking, others joined in. Someone said the committee needed to determine the duties and role of the Head of Digital Systems. Another person asked if we really needed a digital systems unit. I looked at my watch. There were twenty-five slides, two minutes per slide for a fifty-minute talk. Their discussion evolved into a debate about policies and procedures, whether the Chief really had the authority to advertise the digital systems position in the first place. Francis sat back with his arms folded. Within less than a week, he formed People for Privacy.

"My project isn't designed to catch thieves. You know that, Henry."

The nerve is acting up again. He darts his hand to his back so quickly you'd think he'd been stung. He squirms in the chair. Then his face relaxes and he continues. "I don't care what your project is designed for anymore than do the People for Privacy. I doubt if anyone cares besides you. Show that your project can stop library theft and people might start to listen."

"You seem to know Blumberg well. Invite him for a visit, have him steal a few hundred books while he's here, why don't you?"

"Wednesday and Friday at 3:45? Same reading carrel every time? Ding, dong, ding, dong. Little Miss Reading Room. You know what's so grand about using her for an example? She's stealing from the Room that Francis Hickey manages. Nab her, and you'll nab him. Then you can advise Mr. Hickey to roll up his petitions, pull down his trousers and wipe his arse with them." He laughs, then coughs up crumbs.

"How were the cookies?" I ask him.

"You mean the chocolate chip biscuits?"

"They're cookies, not biscuits. Biscuits have nowhere near the number of calories."

"You're the one who does all the counting and what bloody good has that done you?" he says.

CHAPTER SEVEN

april's grudge

Always on Wednesday and Friday, always at 3:45, always in the same reading carrel. Henry and I skip our afternoon coffee for one day so I can pay a visit to the Room. Other reading rooms I've visited or seen in pictures have wall-to-wall rows of tables and chairs. They should call them study halls. The Special Collections Reading Room isn't a study hall. It's more like four cozy salons without walls between them. Each one has chairs, a couch, table and a large secretary that Henry and I call reading carrels.

**Welcome to the Special Collections Reading Room,
KING EDWARD UNIVERSITY LIBRARY**

1. No food, drinks, chewing gum, talking, rubbings of bindings, corrector fluid, highlighter pens, cameras, cellphones, headsets or personal scanners.

2. Patrons may consult no more than one item at a time.

3. Maximum reading period: three consecutive hours.

4. Materials may be consulted only in the Room.

3:45. She passes in front of me, leans on the main counter, picks up a request slip then fills it in. She's much taller than I thought. From my office, I hadn't noticed the rusty-coloured freckles, blue eyes, wind-burned face or the single purple streak in her silky black hair. She's dressed for April weather that's behaving like the middle of winter. Makes me think of someone holding a grudge for too long.

She completes the slip then slides it across the counter to the clerk. He swivels round and disappears into the stacks. While she waits, she sheds layers of windbreaker, scarf and woollen sweater. Strands of her hair stand on end when her sweater comes off. Our eyes meet for such a pithy instant I'm tempted to believe it didn't happen. The clerk hands her a folder, she signs the slip then goes to her carrel.

I lick my fingers, run them through my hair and think: write – *buy comb* on my priority list. "Hello," I say to the clerk. "I'm Carl Brunet, Head of Digital Library Systems here at the library. Part of my job involves analyzing and interpreting library user data, such as what people put on request slips. Could I glance at that slip?"

"You're that Bibliosomething dude I read about in the *Campus Voice*."

The reporter got it all wrong. As part of the explanation about my project, I'd said that if he lived in London he'd be caught on public surveillance cameras about three hundred times per day. My point was that we need to come to terms with the fact that we live in an information society. He shook my hand after the interview. "Good luck," he said. I thought the article would be positive publicity for the library. Not so. The headline read: *Big Brother at the King E.*

"It's Bibliomining, actually. What about the slip? Could I have a moment with it?"

"I guess," he says. "If it's part of your work, then it's OK." He

hands me the request slip, a strip of paper and pencil.

I check over my shoulder. She's still in her carrel.

Name: Dr. Norah Myrick
Faculty/Department: History
Office: A4005
Tel. no.: 737-2335
ID.: Faculty: 900034258
Manuscript title: H. Mainwaring papers
Format: Folder of loose pages (Approx. 50)
Original publication date: 1622
Library user number: 007440982
Date/Time out: 04/15/2000 15:50
Time returned:

He watches me as if he's trying to learn how to do it. I slide the slip away from him. He follows along after me. "What's the name of that group again? What's the expression they have? It was in the newspaper."

I was on my way to work one morning. A young woman, probably no more than a first or second year student, asked me if I wanted a pen. She was giving them away outside the entrance. I took two. One had the slogan: *Privacy not prying*. The other said: *Keep your nose out of my book*. That was how the People for Privacy launched their campaign.

I pose the pencil and the card on the counter. "I'm not sure. Thank you." I smile then walk away. I have one last glance before I leave. She's in her usual spot in the corner. I walk past the notice board on my way to the exit. *Our digital camera (without flash) is available for use. We scan maps on demand. Consider making a donation to the Newfoundlandia fund. Sign Now.* I follow an arrow that points to a petition.

Did you know an attorney in the southern U.S.A.
demanded that a library turn over the borrowing

histories of its patrons? The attorney was trying to solve a case of child abandonment. He wanted the names of every person who had borrowed books on childbirth.

Could this happen at King Edward University Library? The People for Privacy believe it could. Sign our petition to demand protection of your right to privacy in the library and everywhere.

New members & donations welcome.
Email us: fhickey@king.nl.ca

If I had a pen, I'd sign *Big Brother*. Instead, I head back to my office, uncrumple the scrap of paper from my pocket then type *Norah Myrick* into my project portal. The portal gives me *carte blanche* access to every major administrative database on campus. I start with circulation. She has 1534 books on loan, mostly on the philosophy of history and historiography. That's nothing. Faculty and graduate students are entitled to unlimited borrowing for unlimited periods. The Human Resources' database shows her age as forty-six; residence, Cliffhead, NL; status, untenured Assistant Professor, History Department. I Google her.

Town Council of Peat Bog Cove
Request by Norah Myrick approved for construction
of a third hexagonal structure at Cliffhead.

The scoremyprofessors.com web site shows three entries:

> *tested us on words to the Ode to Newfoundland.*
> *Hello? Anybody there?*
> *rubber-booted tree-hugger with a Nfld flag draped*
> *over her shoulders. Avoid!!!*
> *fair markr Midterm wz a joke Final WZ CRAP*

An Imperfect Librarian

I program the database to alert me of additions or changes related to the name Norah Myrick. Next, I open a word-processing document to record the information I've gathered so far. I name the file francis_norah.doc.

afternoon worry break

I CAN'T BLAME HENRY FOR WANTING to sit nearer the window. He's so short he needs a front row seat to be able to see down into the Room. There's a hooded body curled up, dozing in a chair. In a nearby carrel, a girl is copying something from a book. The couple on the two-seater couch below the window are necking. Straight ahead, a long rectangular beam of light cuts through the greens, blues and reds in the stained glass.

"Can you move away from the window and be less obvious about it?"

"Less obvious about what?" Henry says.

I don't bother to argue. I rearrange the chairs while Henry serves himself at the stand. He walks his fingers through the cookies, picks a plump one then goes to his chair. I pour my own cup, wipe off the stand and circle round to join him. By then, he's already rearranged the seating and the conversation. "Your libido is a) in remission, b) in quarantine, c) on extended disability leave or d) in some other arrested state. Which one?" he says.

I take my place next to him. "How would you feel if your wife left you for another woman?"

"I wouldn't marry that type of woman."

"It's not that simple."

"That's because you make everything more complicated than it needs to be," he says.

"I was a good husband. I did everything I could to please her."

For her thirty-fifth birthday I borrowed some money to buy tickets for two to Greece. I tried to come up with the best itinerary, best hotels, best gift, best husband. I put the tickets in a large box and had it gift-wrapped. We went out to supper. As planned, the waiter came by with the box during dessert. Diners at other tables turned to view the spectacle. I watched her face. She smiled and laughed as she pulled out fat wads of stuffing. Her expression changed when she found the tickets in an envelope at the bottom. It turned out Elsa didn't want to go to Greece. She'd been there already.

"There are husbands who are pathological cheats," Henry says. "There are husbands who are pathological liars. Then there's the worst kind." He pauses as if he's expecting me to finish his sentence.

"What's that?" I ask.

"The pathologically pleasing husbands," he says.

"More like pathologically wrong. I worried that she'd leave me for another man, not another woman."

"Is worrying the strategy you have in mind for dealing with Francis and his People for Privacy?" he says.

"I need a break from conversations about Francis."

"A break from worrying about him, did you mean?"

"Whatever."

"If worrying didn't prevent your wife from leaving you, don't expect it to work with Francis. All you'll accomplish is a self-fulfilling prophecy."

"I hate those words. You sound like Elsa."

When she came home late night after night, I couldn't resist questioning her: Where were you? Why does it matter? It matters to me. I was nowhere. You had to have been somewhere. Who cares? I care. You're such a bore sometimes, Carl. Yes, well please remember you're married to the bore.

"You ended up instigating exactly what you feared most," Henry says.

"The more I worried about her leaving me, the more she pulled away, the more she pulled away, the more I worried, and so on and so on. I went alone to a psychologist as a final resort. Elsa wouldn't come. 'You're the one with the problem,' she said."

"I'm surprised someone who counts his pennies the way you do would tolerate paying psychologists' fees," Henry says. "I would have diagnosed you for far less." He eases up from his chair like a woman pregnant with twins who stands with the shape of the chair still under her. He takes three or four steps before he can straighten up completely. His gait is awkward because the sciatic nerve problem makes his left leg move slightly to the side each time he steps forward. He compensates with the movement of his right leg or else he might go sideways instead of forward.

I slide both our chairs away from the window. "And what would you have diagnosed?"

He returns with a refill. Matter-of-factly, he lays it on my desk as he moves his chair back where it was. "We haven't discussed my fee yet," he says. "Give me a précis of the diagnosis and move up here to the front so I don't have to pay for conversation with a sprained neck."

I slide my chair forward next to his. "The psychologist figured I was clinging to my wife because I was afraid she'd abandon me like my mother did."

"What does your mother have to do with anything?"

I shrug my shoulders. "I'm the patient, not the psychologist. What do I know?"

"Not much by the sound of things. What you need is a good shag to take your mind off your worries. And when you are worrying, it shouldn't be about a wife who wasn't attracted to the opposite sex. Not when you've got Francis spitting in your face."

"I think Elsa cares for me. She's simply passing through a premature mid-life crisis. One of these days, I'll open up my email and there'll be a message from her."

"What are you expecting that email to offer? 'Hi, Carl. Come back to Norway at once. I've decided I'm not a lesbian anymore. I want to give you a blow job *tout de suite.*'"

"I don't care what the email says. I simply need to believe there's hope."

"Put your hope in a basket alongside your worrying, pour some petrol over the lot and set it ablaze. Your delusional hoping is worse than your festered, infected worrying. The sooner you clue into that fact, the sooner you'll be feeling like a new man."

"That's more or less what the psychologist said. And what good did that do me?"

"But I'm not a psychologist."

"Then what qualifies you to speak with such authority?"

He shakes his head. "You don't need a psychologist to see what's wrong with you any more than you need a meteorologist to advise you to open or close your umbrella when it's raining."

"All right. I forget about her. Then what?"

"Put your energy into dealing with Francis. Before you know it, you won't remember her name."

"You make it sound too easy."

He nods again then raises the type of hand that bestows a blessing. "You have me to guide you."

"Thanks, Henry. If you didn't have such a fat belly, I'd put my arms around you and hug you."

He leans away from me. "If you weren't such a fragile, fucking wimp, I'd give you a boot in the arse."

CHAPTER NINE

the loose-knit librarian

ELSA'S STAY IN ENGLAND WAS supposed to last a year or *until* she managed better in English. She was working as a waitress *until* she found a better job. Her flat was rented by the month *until* she could afford a better place. I followed her to Norway where she agreed to *until* death do us part, which evolved into *until* Brutus do us part. Elsa called her Sophie. They did lots together: went to the gym, talked on the phone, skied, and attended a judo competition in Stockholm for five days. They worked in the same travel agency.

Brutus showed up at our Oslo flat one day. "Come with me now, Elsa, or it's over," she said. I listened to them quarrel. *What's over?* I wanted to ask. For months after, I walked past her flat and office daily until I wore the pavement thin. It was also Brutus' flat and office. Whenever I called or emailed, she answered.

Norway felt overcrowded all of a sudden. I considered moving back to London but there'd be far too many memories of Elsa. Tatie didn't live there anymore. England was a country of uncultured monarchists without manners or taste. That's what she told me after she moved back to France to live with Papa. She wanted me to move there too. "Come home and take care of us," she said. If it hadn't been for the ad in the librarian's journal, I might have done exactly that.

KING EDWARD UNIVERSITY LIBRARY,
St. John's, Newfoundland, Canada,
invites applications for the permanent position of
Head of Digital Library Systems.
Preference may be given to bilingual applicants.

Appointment effective September, 1999.
For information, visit: http://king.nl.ca/HR/library

I applied and waited. The longer I waited, the more I dreaded the possibility that I'd spend the rest of my life in Norway. When they finally offered me the position, I dreaded the thought of being so far away from her. The day before I left, I stopped by Elsa's new flat. I should have known Brutus would be there. It was the first time I'd seen her that close. I counted the number of piercings and stopped after five. Her forehead was riddled with pockmarks. Her hair stood hard, like bristles on a scrub brush. Elsa had left me for an inferior being. What did that make me?

She was in the bathroom when I arrived. I sat opposite Brutus in the living room. There was no music or radio, no sound besides our breathing. I flipped through a *Bodybuilding for Women* magazine. *Positive Steroid Use and Testosterone Supplements.* I heard the click of the bathroom door behind me. Elsa leaned over the back of my chair to give me a peck on the cheek then sat with Brutus on the couch. The two of them cuddled together and held hands. Brutus tilted her head to kiss Elsa's ear.

The conversation was about "we" except "we" didn't include me. "We're going on holiday to Greece," she said. "It was a surprise gift from Sophie for my birthday."

Up until then, Elsa had done all the talking.

"When I invited you, you claimed it was too Greek," I said. "But when Brutus invites you it's a special voyage. What's changed?"

"Nothing has changed. I've always been Sophie, not Brutus."

"Elsa, could we talk alone without her interrupting?"

"Say what you want. There are no secrets between Sophie and me. We—"

"Please, Elsa. Ask her to go. I'm leaving tomorrow for Canada. I may never return. It's a permanent position." I stood up then reached forward to take Elsa's hand. "I want to talk to Elsa alone," I said to Brutus.

Brutus shoved her fist against my chest. That's when I noticed the *ELSA* tattoo, one letter per knuckle. I stumbled over the side table and nearly fell.

"Why do you always insist?" Elsa said. "Why can't you accept that I'm with Sophie?"

I couldn't answer those questions then or now. I sent her one last email hoping she'd come to the airport to say goodbye:

Flight 205 to London @ 22:30. I'll wait at the Air Norway counter. Do **NOT** tell Brutus. Please!

I checked my mail at an Internet station before I boarded the plane. I was relieved to find a message I thought came from Elsa:

Date: Wed. August 30 1999 21:42
To: carlbrunet@hotmail.com
From: elsa60@hotmail.com

Elsa has no feeling for you except pity. LEAVE HER ALONE!

Sophie

After that night, the only response I received from my emails to Elsa was *Message blocked for this recipient.* If I'd been nice to Brutus, she might have allowed Elsa to come see me at the airport, but being nice to her wasn't something I could pretend under any circumstances. And so I headed off to the end of the world, overwhelmed with longing for my wife and loathing for her lover. Someone at the library arranged temporary accommodation for me in a basement flat in St. John's. The owners, Mercedes and her husband Cyril, were a couple in their late fifties, volunteers with the newcomers' society. They met me at the airport. *Welcome, Carl Brunet,* their sign read.

Cyril spoke first, very quickly. "How ya gettin' on?"

"Sorry?" I responded.

"How are you?" he said.

Later, when we knew each other better, Cyril confessed he was concerned. "I don't know who knit you, but you were some slow catching on that night at the airport."

At the time, I didn't expect to be around them for long. "Thanks for the flat," I said. "My wife will be joining me soon. We'll be needing a larger place then."

CHAPTER TEN

a fishy resolution

I MOVED TO NEWFOUNDLAND THINKING IT would distract me until Elsa and I could work things out. In the meantime, I planned to plunge myself into implementing my vision for the library of the future – omniscient, ubiquitous and with all the knowledge of the world at our fingertips. The plunge was more like a duck-n-cover. The vision was more like a blind spot. People misunderstood my role. I wasn't there to help the administration cut jobs by computerising services. I had no plan to siphon the library's book budget in order to purchase computers. Contrary to what Francis was claiming, I was not engaged in any form of electronic surveillance.

Mercedes and Cyril were guardian angels, especially during the first few months. If it hadn't been for their hospitality, I might have headed back to Norway. They invited me for supper every third or fourth night. After we'd eaten, we'd play 120s or watch the news. I'd take the La-Z-Boy chair. They'd sit on the couch. By 9:30, she'd be asleep with her feet in his lap. Cyril's head would be plopped forward and he'd be snoring into his chest. At that point, I'd open the basement door to go downstairs to my flat.

I spent Christmas with them and their daughter, Heather while she was home from university. Cyril gave me a fishing rod as a gift. "We'll go troutin' on the May 24th weekend," he told me. Night after night, we played a trivia game. Cyril and I formed one team against Mercedes and Heather. I was good with literature. He knew all the answers in the sports categories. Mercedes and Heather beat us every time.

It was my second Christmas without Elsa. For the first one, she was with Brutus. I asked her if she'd come by. I told her about the gift I'd bought. She said maybe Christmas morning. I had everything ready, decorated our tree, bought some eggnog, put a ribbon on the bike. Every time a car pulled up I'd jump up to look out the window. By 4:00 in the afternoon, I turned off the Christmas lights. I ate some curried turkey from the corner store then drank half the bottle of wine with the card that said: *all my love, Carl*. When I woke it was December 26th.

Mercedes and Cyril weren't the only ones who helped me after I arrived in Newfoundland. Edith went out of her way to do things for me. She made sure I had lunch every day. She told me I should get out more, buy some new clothes, and find a proper living situation for a man my age. When I told Henry about her shoulds, he said Edith and I would make a fine pair. "She wouldn't get shagged in a bucketful of pricks and you wouldn't know a tit if it introduced itself to you."

During my first month at the library, Edith spent more time in my office than her own. After a while, I had to stop leaving my door ajar. But then she'd knock; I'd answer and she'd come in. Henry and I eventually settled on a coded knock-knock-knock-knock, one of those quick, successive, galloping horse beats, four times in a row.

Henry was also very helpful during the first few months

and after. He drove me around everywhere and even lent me his car. Eventually, I thought it was time I bought one of my own. He came with me to help pick it out. I told him, "Thanks, Henry, I'll make the final decision." I turned to the salesman in his eager-for-the-deal white shirt and skinny black leather tie to shake his hand.

Before I could open my mouth, Henry bumped against me, hands in his pockets, and announced loud enough for the salesman to hear, "It's a deflated, impotent prick of a car. You're wasting your fucking money. It'll be a worse pain in the arse than a severe case of haemorrhoids."

I bought the car. It was a lemon. Henry was right. But that didn't justify his behaviour with the salesman. I told him that and he said I was a thumb-sucking sissy. The more time I spend in his company, the more I worry about his behaviour. Although, I wouldn't be surprised if he's thinking the same about me.

He did make it easier during those initial months when I thought I'd made a mistake moving to Newfoundland. I wasn't going to run into Elsa walking down the street in St. John's. I couldn't go to her flat to ask her why she wasn't answering my mail or my calls. It wasn't only Elsa I missed. Tatie and Papa were getting older and more dependent on me. The Oslo to Paris flight was quick and cheap. From there, I used to take the train to the nearby town where they'd pick me up in their car. I couldn't do that as easily anymore now that I was on the other side of the ocean.

For the first few months after I arrived in Newfoundland, Tatie called almost daily to talk about her news, local news, international news, no news. "I only wanted to say hello," she'd say. "Is it all right to call you at work? Are you busy?" I was never too busy to talk to her. Mostly, she talked. I listened. "I hope you'll be moving back to this side of the world soon..." Some days the calls went on for a very long time. "I told the man at the market I would never pay that price for aubergines, not if I was a millionaire but…" I was glad to hear that she was taking an interest in what was going on in their village. "Maximillian's wife had her surgery. She's doing well…"

Tatie worried about me. She worried about Papa too. Especially about his memory. She told me about an incident when he was making rice. He boiled the kettle, then dropped the bouillon cube inside. Tatie warned him he'd spoil the kettle if he dissolved the cube in there. He ignored her. Months later, he was making a dish that called for bouillon cube. She held out the kettle to him.

"I'm not going to put the cube in there," he said. "That will ruin the kettle. What's wrong with you, Georgette?" When she argued with him, he told her she was losing her mind.

Tatie never had any children of her own. Papa said it was because the French weren't meant to mate with the English. When her English husband Philip left her, she clung to me like I was the last child on earth. Even when I was no longer a child, she insisted that I stay with her. "You can't leave me alone. You're all I have." When I turned thirty, she decided it was time for me to move out. "Find a wife," she told me. I was almost forty by the time that happened.

I brought photos of them with me to Newfoundland on my laptop. Elsa was in nearly all of them including those with Tatie and Papa. I had taken hundreds of shots of her during our trip to Egypt. There were before and after renovation pictures of our flat. I also had various photos of her important moments: at her third-place road race win, first day on the job at the travel agency, posing with her guru yoga teacher.

When Mercedes realized I had photos of my life in France, England and Norway, she wanted to see them. I started with the Tatie-Papa photos. Next, we looked at some photos of Elsa. After about fifty, Mercedes said she had something to show me. She hurried off to another room while I sat back on the La-Z-Boy and watched the local news with Cyril. She returned during a Central Dairies commercial.

"Let me help you with those," I told her.

She unloaded the albums into my arms. It didn't take her long to find the photo she was searching for. "That's my friend Nancy," she said. "She's a nurse too. There's tons of fish in the ocean, you know." After that incident, whenever they invited me for supper there'd be another woman sitting by my side. First there was Nancy, then Sharon, Heather, same Nancy, Patricia, Carol, Nancy again.

For New Year's, I went with Mercedes and Cyril to the harbour-front. It was so jammed with people that I lost sight of the two of them not long after we arrived. The revellers huddled together under a sky with a shiny black marble finish. The clock ticked down, people chanted *five, four, three…* fireworks exploded. The ships' horns blasted and echoed off the surrounding hills. People I didn't know hugged me, shook my hand or shoved against me. Then, someone grabbed me from behind. It was Mercedes. She wrapped her arms around me. "We're some glad you're with us," she said. Cyril gave me a friendly smack on the shoulder.

"Now's the time for resolutions," Mercedes announced. Cyril resolved to finish installing the clapboard on the house, Mercedes resolved to not nag him anymore about the clapboard, and, for lack of a better idea, I resolved to do more fishing. Mercedes winked at me.

Cyril said, "I was thinking we should rent us a place up in Terra Nova National Park for that May 24th weekend and…"

I'd never felt a wind as cold as what rolled down between the hills to the harbour-front that night. Somehow, though, I didn't mind. People told me I'd get used to the weather on the island and I guess they were right.

CHAPTER ELEVEN

d is for duckies

THE DAYS DRAG INTO WEEKS, the weeks drag into months, the months drag me forward. I pretend to be listening during meetings where they ramble on about e-solutions, e-learning, e-searching, e-libraries when all I care about is e-lsa. I adjust to life on a barren island, to the foreign Newfoundland accents, to the unconscious kindness of the locals. I don't adjust to being so far away from Elsa, yet so close to knowing that she may never leave Brutus. I'm tired of opening my email to find the usual *Message blocked for this recipient.*

Six months on the opposite side of the ocean and the closest I've come to an email from her is one with an E in the sender line. The sender is Edith.

> *We should go for a beer after work today. What*
> *do you say?*
> *Edie*
> *xoxox*
> *P.S. Careful. In your last email, you had "there"*
> *books. Should be "their" books.*

We meet in the library lobby then walk to the Campus Quaff where it's standing room only. Edith nudges so close to me you'd swear we were two of twenty sardined into an elevator. Before long, a group of people leave. Edith swoops down on two vacated chairs. We sit together, elbows touching.

"See her?" Edith says. She reaches her hand in front of my face to point at someone at the opposite table. "Remember Paul Hiscock? The man I introduced you to in the campus cafeteria? The one who's married to the secretary of the director of the library's financial section? That's his wife."

"How can she be his wife if he's married to the secretary of whatever?"

"He's married to the secretary of the director of the library's financial section."

"Is this a conversation about bigamy?" I joke.

"What are you talking about?"

"That's exactly what I'm asking you?"

"You're asking me if the conversation is about bigamy?"

"Forget it, Edith. It's not important."

I do speak the same language as people in Newfoundland, at least in theory, so I should be able to get my meaning across but I don't. It's worse when I try to be funny. I've been trying hard since I arrived in Newfoundland. Everyone else here seems to be a natural with it. Cyril's been giving me lessons. He thinks I'm catching on.

Edith and I watch the crowd while we wait for a waitress to serve us. A group of people is heading towards the door. That's when I notice her. "Do you know that woman just leaving? The one with the shoulder-length black hair and yellow raincoat?"

"Norah Myrick?" Edith says. "The last time I laid my eyes on her, she was downtown, in a bar, smack dab in the centre of the dance floor slithering like a snake. Mr. Myrick wouldn't have approved."

"Her husband?"

"Jesus, Mary and Smallwood! No. Her father, William Myrick. Patron saint of Newfoundland books. That man knew more about the millions of items in the archives and Reading Room than all of us put together. God love him. He was working on a book. He'd say, Edie dear, tell me the truth, Edie, what do you think of this title? My favourite was *Memories of a Silent Voice: The Written Tradition in Eighteenth and Nineteenth Century Rural Newfoundland*. He used to travel to the outports collecting every scrap of written material he could put his eyes on: diaries, ships' logs, journals, pamphlets, store ledgers, notebooks, letters, you name it."

The waitress interrupts. We study the menu: *deep-fried cod, deep-fried shrimp, deep-fried cod tongues, deep-fried chicken, deep-fried squid, deep-fried onion rings*. We place our order.

"Have I ever seen Mr. Myrick in the library?"

"Not unless you're seeing ghosts," she says. "You might hear stories about him though."

"You mean he was a saint with a sin?"

"I didn't bother signing things out for him when he came to the archives. I knew what he had. He liked to work in the evening. We closed at five so he'd bring home what he needed. He'd been coming to the archives for years. He donated huge amounts of materials. They didn't know him in the Reading Room like I did. Students take care of the dealings with the customers nowadays. Part-timers, most of them are. They don't know our regulars. We'll all be replaced by students sooner or later. God help us."

The waitress returns with our drinks, fish and chips. Edith waves to people.

"So what was his sin?"

"He was working in the Reading Room at the time. At the end of the day, he dropped whatever he was working on into his briefcase then walked out the door. He didn't go far. The alarm nearly gave him a heart attack. He told me that on the phone after. The student-clerk tried to take his briefcase. William smacked him right across the head with it. He wasn't allowed within fifty feet of the campus after that. It's a shame. You know another thing that's a shame? You sitting so far from me. Move over closer. Don't be so unfriendly."

The bartender calls out, "Happy Hour, five to seven."

"That's Great Big Sea's music," Edith says. "You can't live in Newfoundland and not be a fan. I'll buy you a CD." She sings along in a high-pitched voice that pays more attention to clear diction than melody. She nudges closer to me, drops her head to touch my shoulder then smiles. "We should do this more often. Why don't we try going out together for a while?"

"I'm not interested in dating right now. Why don't you speak to Henry?"

"Don't insult me, please," she says.

"What's wrong with Henry?"

She adds salt and vinegar to her chips. "You should know. You spend enough time with him."

"I rely on him for advice and–"

"Don't let yourself be influenced by him. When administration announced they were advertising the digital systems position, he threatened to stage a one-man strike. If he had his way, you wouldn't be here."

The steam is rising off the gravy. I grab a chip and pop it in my mouth. "I don't blame him for feeling threatened. If the Internet takes off, eventually we won't need Information Services Librarians anymore. We'll have interactive support built into the software with the searching capacity and skill of thousands–"

"The only thing Henry should feel threatened by is the administration. If they could be rid of him, they would. If he's not careful, he'll give them grounds that even the union won't be able to help him with."

"Such as?"

"He's rude to the students. If they don't know what he thinks they should, he insults them. Remember our creed. A is for access, B is for borrowing, U is for understanding. We're expected to have as much knowledge of our readers as we do of books. He's an embarrassment to the profession."

"I'm sure he was a great librarian in his earlier days. I've never met anyone with such passion for books and reading."

"That'd be fine and dandy if he'd share his passion with library patrons, but he doesn't. Not unless it's one of those darling young duckies with the bulges in the right places."

For Valentine's Day, he had given a rose to every woman on staff. I saw the red flowers on desks and counters all over the library, with a card that read, *Be mine, Valentine! HK.*

"Henry is lonely."

"More like lecherous," she says as she reaches for the ketchup.

He once told me he longed for a Spanish or Italian woman, a long-haired brunette with tight cleavage and a heart that's warm as the nicest of grandmothers on a Sunday.

"He has no family here. He's in pain constantly because of his sciatic nerve. He's frustrated with the changes in his role, changes in the–"

"Why are you defending him?" she says.

"Why not? He watches out for me."

She places her hand on top of mine. "I watch out for you too."

Someone she knows comes to the table to chat. After they leave, I dig into my fish and chips while Edith launches into her plans for my first summer on the island. "We'll drive across the island, go to Gros Morne, climb the mountain. It's a world heritage site. We could stay in B&Bs if you're not the camping type."

"I don't have any holidays accumulated yet. Remember, I came here in September and it's only April."

"You're allowed statutory holidays. That would give us three long weekends. We could visit the archaeological site at Ferryland. We'll have a ball."

"I didn't say I was going."

"You'll change your mind once summer comes and I show up at your office, all tanned, in my shorts and hiking boots – the sun splitting the rocks, the air filled with the smoke and smell of barbecues, the bugs and fish biting."

If I have my way, I'll be back with Elsa by then.

CHAPTER TWELVE

a meaty morsel of a miracle

I T'S THE TIME OF YEAR in England people call spring: tulips already faded, lilacs about to blossom, Easter bonnets stored away. In Newfoundland, the tulips are still in hibernation, icebergs are dotting shorelines, studded snow tires and skidoos are not yet stored away. The snow has melted and left the city littered with discarded coffee cups, lost mittens and scarves – as if we needed proof that the winter storms were so strong they'd blow the clothes off your back. For my fiftieth birthday, Mercedes and Cyril gave me a t-shirt with the caption: *I survived the winter of '99-2000* under a sketch of someone holding a shovel next to a snowbank.

Inside my office, without an exterior window, the only sign of spring is the change in Henry's mood. He's more determined than ever that he'll convince a woman to go on a date with him before the summer comes. If his track record is any indication of future success, I'd encourage him not to get his hopes up.

"She told me to check with her fiancé," Henry says. "What does a darling like her want with a husband?"

"What did Mrs. Kelly want with her Henry?"

"I would never have wed in the first place, but her breasts made more than my eyes bulge. All the lads wanted to feel her up. When her Da caught us, he gave me two choices: marry her or marry her. I chose the latter. I was eighteen and almost as clueless as you are."

"How was it?"

"Grand at first," he says. "Sex to die for, unlimited quantities. After three babies in less than four years, I didn't want sex anymore. All I cared about was one measly moment of calm alone with a book, without the howling, crying, fighting and the Jesus-knows-whatever-else I suffered for too long. When the children grew up and moved out, Mrs. Henry Kelly went with them. Mister accepted a job at a library in Canada where he's been celebrating the respite from the storm ever since."

"You know what I think?"

He shakes his head. "I couldn't possibly fathom the likes of your mind, Carl."

I pretend to be watching the Room. "I think there's a woman waiting for you out there."

He glances at me sideways.

"She's eager, pleasing and just down the hall."

He abandons his usual slouch and widens his eyes. "Who?" he asks.

I cross my legs then sit back in my chair as if the topic wasn't really that important. "The woman of your dreams."

"Who?"

I turn to face him. "Edith."

He resumes his deflated position in his chair with his hands folded over his belly. "You can inform her on my behalf that she's wasting her precious time."

"Why not? She's smart, she knows tons of people, she's–"

He shoos me with the back of his hand. "Invite her out

yourself if you're so crazy about her," he says.

"Have you ever considered dating Edith?"

"She's not on my radar. Besides, I'm attracted to cleavage. Hers is about as well-defined as yours."

I look down at my chest. "Stop that, Henry. People will start talking about us."

"That'd be a blessing for you – give them something else to gossip about besides your conspiracy to spy on them with your databases and Bibliomining Project."

"That's not what I'm doing with my project. You know that."

He leans away from me. "Ease off. They're the ones claiming conspiracy, not me. I don't care if you're conspiring. Do what you want. I'm only trying to resuscitate you."

I turn in my chair to face him. "What do you expect to receive in exchange?"

"Half-decent coffee. Could be better. The view. If you'd give me the binoculars. You're my charity case, my volunteer work, my university service. We're expected to do a certain amount. I dare say you've exceeded my quota."

I shake my head. "I'm not counting."

"You're not doing *anything* worthwhile. Francis is chasing after you. Meanwhile you're too busy crawling on your hands and knees after your Scandinavian princess to care about anything else."

"I do care. I simply have to deal with Elsa first."

"You don't have time. Francis is rallying the troops. His war-cry has a distinctive anti-Brunet tone. Haven't you heard his privacy ditty? It goes to the tune of 'Yankee Doodle.'" Henry abandons his usual slouch. He sings the ditty with his hands on his waist, elbows pointed out to the sides. "Biblio Brunet spies on us, using a computer. Hide your files, watch your back. He's an information looter. Or do you prefer something to the tune of 'Camptown Races'? I always liked the Doo-da, Doo-da in the song." For this one, he sways side to side to mark the rhythm.

"Don't let Brunet spy on you, on you, on you. Don't let Brunet see your files, any time of day. He's a bumbling fool, drowning in his drool. Don't let Brunet see your files, any time of day. What do you think, Carl?"

"I think you shouldn't joke about it."

"What would you know about joking?"

"My project is not proposing anything anyone has to fear."

"Francis' prime strategy's making people afraid. What's your strategy? Or are you going to watch him undermine you while you waste away after your princess? What exactly are your priorities again?"

"They're fighting with each other, scrambling for first place."

He raises his fingers in my face. "Priority number one: deal with Francis." He raises a second finger. "Priority number two: deal with Francis."

"I did a search of his name in the database. *Information not found. Try refining your search.* That's all I got."

He laughs. "Try refining your search. There's a meaty morsel of advice for a man in your condition. Search for a miracle, or, at the minimum, for some sense to sort out the mess you're in."

"Half or quarter of a miracle would do. Anything for Elsa to contact me. Once she does, I'll manage from there."

Henry shakes his head before he rises from his seat. "Why do I bother? Especially on a day like today when the view is below average and the coffee has the texture of sandpaper because you're too cheap to buy proper filters. If you want to waste your miracle on Elsa instead of Francis, I don't give a shit what happens to you."

"Thanks for the reassurance of your friendship."

"No additional charge," he says.

A MEATY MORSEL OF A MIRACLE

robinson crusoe revisited

I T's THE END OF A dragged-out day that started late. Most people have gone home. The Reading Room is dark. I sign out of the databases then put the lid on the cookie tin. I count them first because I have a suspicion that the night cleaners, security, whoever, are pilfering them when I'm not around. The phone rings. It can't be Henry. He wouldn't call this time of day. Tatie and Papa would be in bed because it's four and a half hours later there. Edith usually emails me or knocks on the door. It could be Mercedes calling to invite me to join them on the weekend for their regular meatloaf and red Jell-O with bananas followed by a game of 120s.

"Hello?"

"It's Elsa. I've been meaning to call you for so long. How are you?"

It *has* been so long. Every time the phone rang for the last year, I hoped it would be her. Every time I opened my email, I searched for her name in the addresses.

"It's Elsa calling you from Oslo. Hello? Carl?"

I haven't forgot how her voice sounds – confident, clear, soft with a sing-songy intonation. I always liked her English accent and the way she pronounces my name as if it has no vowels.

"Carl? Are you there?"

"Hello, Elsa. Yes. It's me."

"I've been meaning to call you but things have been hectic here. How are you, Carl? What have you been doing? Tell me your news about your new job, your flat, everything."

"Flat's nice. Job's great. I'm getting used to the weather. How have you been?"

"There's not too much to tell. Thank you for the birthday gift. I was going to send you a note. Mother and Father gave me new ski equipment. They were skiing a lot this year." She sighs. "They're growing older, like me. How is your health?"

"My colleague Edith invites me for meals occasionally. She's only my colleague. There's nothing between us or anything."

"You know it's so important to eat well, especially as we grow older, especially for women when they reach a certain age. Like me. It's a worry sometimes, growing old and wondering who'll care for us. Do you ever think about that, Carl?"

"Yes. I do."

"My parents are so lucky. They have me to take care of them. I'm not surprised that they're asking when I will have children. I am not too old yet but in a few years…"

We had talked about being a *mor* and *far* with *datter, sønn* or both. I couldn't see myself as a *far* but if that's what Elsa wanted, I was only too willing to make her happy.

"…I don't want to adopt, not when I could have the baby myself, not when I still have a healthy husband and I'm a healthy woman who…"

Elsa was proud of me when we first married. I'd won a scholarship to go to graduate school. Elsa hadn't gone to university. In school she excelled in the gym and slept in the classroom.

"...and I want to have the experience of giving birth. Do you understand me?"

"Of course, you want to have the baby yourself."

"You always said you'd do anything for me and I knew you were sincere. I remember when you said..."

I had tried to be the way she wanted me: more talkative, more affectionate, more outgoing, more assertive, more athletic. I could be agile with a database. I was a power-lifter for numbers, flexible with scientific concepts. I could manoeuvre my way through the most complex electronic library systems, yet I'd trip over my own feet if I jogged or played ball sports.

"This is what I'm calling you about. You did say you'd do anything for me, right?"

"Yes, Elsa."

"Oh, Carl. You are such a sweetheart. Marlene said you were like a puppy. Do you remember Marlene? She has two girls now. They're adorable. By the time the first one was five months old..."

Elsa had plenty of friends. I didn't have much time for socializing while I was studying.

"...but I wouldn't want to have two girls. A boy and a girl would be nice. What do you think?"

"I haven't really thought about it."

"A son with a father like you and a mother like me would be tall, intelligent, athletic. What colour hair do you think he'd have?"

"What colour would you like?"

"Can we do it?"

"Do what?"

"Make a child like this?"

"You mean hypothetically?"

"I'm forty, Carl. You can't imagine how much I want to do this. I think of nothing else—"

"Don't cry, Elsa. I didn't know this was so important to you. I'm sorry."

"Can we make a child?"

"You mean you want to have a baby with me as the father?"

"Please, Carl. Don't say no to me. Do it as my husband. Do it for me, please!"

"Yes, Elsa. We can talk about it—"

"Thank you. I knew I could count on you. I hope you won't mind if Sophie shares in our happiness. She's like you in many ways. She'd do anything for me. She wants a family as much as I do. We could arrange it for July. That means the baby would be born near Easter next year. What do you think?"

I think, What will Henry say when he learns that after so much hoping, wanting, longing, wishing, all I have to show is an opportunity to share paternity with Brutus? Instead of responding with anger, I opt for reason. "I think what you're asking me to do is screw myself. I decline the offer." End of call.

My computer screensaver alternates through an Elsa slideshow. A photo of the two of us on a ferry fades onto the screen. It was the day we moved from England to Norway. There's a photo of Elsa's athletic body sprawled the length of our divan. That was earlier in our marriage, before she stopped spending time at home.

Segments of the conversation replay themselves like a refrain: *impregnate me, family, baby.* I activate the screensaver controls, locate a folder named *Elsa,* then press delete. The message box responds with: *Are you sure you want to delete Elsa? Yes or no?* I press Y, wait three seconds, find the recycle bin, empty the recycle bin. End of instructions, end of Elsa. Next, I dispense with the honeymoon photo by sending

Mr. and Mrs. Brunet sailing on a swift voyage across my office, smack into the wall.

The fresh air on the walk from the library to the parking lot revives me. I feel less nauseated. The car coughs and chokes but doesn't start. My breath condenses on the windshield. I trace the sum with the tip of my finger: $-3 + -6 + -2 = -11$. Minus two equals the number of years (rounded off to the nearest black whole) that I wasted after she left. I should have clued in long before that, like during the three years together before our six years of marriage. I breathe in deeply, then exhale onto the glass. Like magic, the sum disappears. Like magic again, the car starts when I turn the key.

I drive to Gower Street and park in front of the house. It's not hard to find, even in the thickest fog. The scaffolding gives it away. Cyril's supposed to be repairing the clapboard when he's not working on building the shed in the back-yard. They celebrated the house's hundredth birthday seven years before I moved into the basement. It still has its original plumbing. Cyril says it's located in the holiest part of the city. The Anglican Cathedral is around the corner. So are the Basilica, the Presentation and Mercy convents. I was waiting to visit them with Elsa.

A cat dashes across the street as if its path is booby-trapped. A man in a baseball hat, jeans and work boots trudges by, leaning under the weight of a stack of empty cases of beer. An orange cab whizzes past, stops and blows its horn. A voice calls from an open door, "Don't forget the loaf of bread." A car pulls up in front of the house. It's Mercedes.

I step out onto the curb. "How was your shift?"

On or off duty, she recognizes a patient. "What happened to you?"

We stand like statues in front of the house, in between the puddles, under the flickering street light. The fog horn groans. Was that an empathetic response? I wonder. I head towards the lane on the side of the house that leads to the basement. "Stomach flu. Don't come too close, Mercedes."

She prescribes ginger ale plus crackers.

I hear her door closing on my way round back. The keyhole in the door of my flat is rusted. I fight with the lock while drops of water drip onto my head. The door opens and I run my fingers along the inside wall to switch on the light. After a shower, I go straight to bed then curl into a ball to conserve heat. I stare at the ceiling. I don't have to stare far because the height is under code at seven rather than the normal eight feet. Cyril claims the basement is warmer that way. "You're a lucky man to have an apartment that heats up so fast," he says. I might be lucky if Cyril turned on the furnace more often. I don't complain about the cold. If they made it any more comfortable, I'd be less inclined to search for a proper place to live. Item number three on my priority list: *find new flat*. It's been high on the list since the day after I arrived in Newfoundland.

My colleagues at the university in Norway warned me life in Newfoundland would be harsh. They were convinced I'd never survive here. They said I'd either be taken hostage by flies just off a hunger strike, pickled from a diet of salted beef, pork and cod, or worse, turned into a native – literally, as in Mohawk with a piercing, fierce cry. They gave me a copy of *Robinson Crusoe* for a going-away gift. On the inside cover they wrote: *Something to read while you're shipwrecked in Newfieland.*

I climb out of bed, go to the closet, open my suitcase then rummage through clothes not worth unpacking. The book is poked in a side pocket with some dirty laundry. I climb under the covers again. My nest is still warm. Defoe's story takes me to the seventeenth century. Crusoe has ignored his father's advice. He's taken to the sea and he's sailing in a storm in the Caribbean. The wind is blowing the ship towards the shore where it will be crushed into a thousand pieces. Before that happens, a mountain of a wave hits. Crusoe is swallowed by the sea. He sinks, but on the last breath, the wave ebbs and leaves him standing on sand. If he can run fast to avoid the second wave, he'll make it to land. If the wave hits him, he knows it can suck him out to sea again. He runs, glancing over his shoulder as he does, but it's too late.

> *The wave that came upon me again buried me at once twenty or thirty feet deep in its own body, and I could feel myself carried with a mighty force and swiftness towards the shore – a very great way; but I held my breath, and assisted myself to swim still forward with all my might. I was ready to burst with holding my breath, when, as I felt myself rising up, so, to my immediate relief, I found my head and hands shoot out above the surface of the water; and though it was not two seconds of time that I could keep myself so, yet it relieved me greatly, gave me breath, and new courage.*

I curl the ear of the page, tuck the book partway under the mattress then turn out the light. It's only a story after all.

CHAPTER FOURTEEN

flavoured accents

NEITHER ELSA'S BETRAYAL NOR CARL'S delusional hoping makes headlines in the following weeks. No state of emergency or day of mourning is proclaimed. People behave as usual and I try to do the same. When I tell Henry about Elsa's call, he says they should establish an award to recognize men like me. "Outstanding-cuckolded-husband-of-all-time award. The recipient has shown evidence of unfailing tenacity in his efforts to cling onto his cheating wife. His superhuman efforts to play the devoted husband earned high esteem for his semen."

I don't have time to gloat over the award. Not when I'm so busy writing reports, reading reports, shredding reports and ordering reports. There's nothing like a report to take your mind off an award, except maybe a meeting. My weekly planner is littered with those. Ordinarily, I reserve the 3:30 to 4:00 block for afternoon break with Henry. Sometimes meetings come up unannounced – which means I have to cancel coffee. Since Henry doesn't use email or voicemail the best way to reach him is to go directly to the booth. He doesn't spend much time in the LAB, so if he's not there, he could be anywhere.

I head to the Information Services booth to change break time from afternoon to morning. Henry is walking away as I arrive. "Be right with you, Carl. The student wants help finding a book on 'metaphorns.' Wait at the booth."

The donut-shaped booth can fit three or four librarians at one time. It's at the centre of a commons area they call the Atrium. When I tilt my head up, I can see the five floors of library stacks. If I were on the top floor looking down, I'd see rows of tables with four chairs on each side. That view will change if my proposal is approved to equip every table with Internet-ready computers.

I browse the booth's computer while I wait. I go to the most interesting part, where the files are too often unorganized. We can create all the information we want, but if we can't effectively access it, what's the point? How can I convince people to be passionate about information management when they don't appreciate proper file–

"Excuse me," she says.

I shift my attention from the screen. The last time I saw her that close was in the Reading Room.

She holds a slip of paper in front of me. "I found this listed in the catalogue. It's supposed to be in the stacks. I checked high, low, under, about, up, down, but it's not there. Can you help me?"

Henry's nowhere in sight. I don't bother searching too hard to find him. "I can try. How about if we visit the stacks?"

We take the elevator to the top floor. We stand side by side facing the door.

"I should be honest, Henry Kelly is the Information Services Librarian on duty, but he's gone off searching for metaphors. I'm a librarian too but I work in another department. You're a historian?" The final n is out. There's no way to undo it.

"How'd you guess?"

"Because of the book you're searching for."

"That's clever," she says.

The elevator jerks upwards then halts. We exit.

"Your accent is English but there's a hint of some other flavour in there that I can't label," she says. "Where're you from? Not Burin, Bonavista or Burgeo surely?"

When Cyril saw me for the first time, he decided instantly that I don't resemble a Newfoundlander. Couldn't explain why. "It's OK, Carl," he said.

"English, yes. Some French. I guess I'd need to be in Newfoundland longer than six or seven months to sound like people do here."

I put up with three years of teasing about my Québécois accent when I arrived in France at five years old. Then Tatie and I moved to England where I put up with taunts about my French accent. Before we left French soil, she warned me that I'd only be allowed to speak English when absolutely required. She forbade any English food in our French diet. I had to eat salad at the end, not before the meal like the English. At school, we had to sing "God Save the Queen" during assemblies. She told me, "There'll be no reverences paid by Carl to English monarchs." Tatie would glance at my school texts then complain that the English were as confused about books as about meals. "Why do they place the table of contents at the beginning and not at the end of their books? Why are they so insensitive to how things should be ordered?"

Norah knows the route better than I do. The truth is I don't know my way around the library except virtually. I can picture the databases down to the most minute detail and file name. I can trace the intricacies of the cataloguing system with my eyes closed. I understand how records are linked, how tags predict users' search habits. But I am, as Henry would argue, "clueless" when it comes to orienting myself in the library stacks.

I make a turn. She heads in the other direction. I backtrack a few steps and follow her again. We're sandwiched between stacks that dwarf us. The book is not where it should be. I browse the shelves above and below. I tilt my head. She does the same. We can't bend far at the waist because we're squat between the narrow stacks. I reach sideways then down too fast; she moves and I smack my skull off hers. I reel back and hit my head again off the edge of the metal book shelf. She raises her hand to my head to stroke it. "I'm so sorry!" she says.

"Don't be sorry. It's not the first time I've hit my head."

From there we head back through the stacks and down in the elevator to the circulation desk to see about the missing book. We're told to talk to a Mrs. Power, but it turns out she's gone for coffee. "Come back in a half-hour," they tell us.

"I could do with a cup of coffee myself right now," Norah says. "How about you? Can I buy you a quick cup?"

I hesitate then nod. The tender hand that stroked my head is the same one I saw through the binoculars from my office.

"My treat – for going beyond the call of duty and being injured in the process. I don't believe we've met officially. I'm Norah. Norah Myrick. History prof, Newfoundlander, woman in search of missing books. You already know so much about me."

We both laugh. For different reasons.

CHAPTER FIFTEEN

behind the curtain of fog

O
N OUR WAY TO THE campus cafeteria, she talks about the Gulf Stream, the Labrador Current and maritime climates of Newfoundland versus the continental climates of central Canada. "The ocean's contrary," she says. "It warms us in the winter, cools us in the summer. I always joke: If the weather doesn't suit you, wait a minute." Cyril had already used that line on me once, but I laugh anyway. We take the university tunnel system. The exposed pipes on the ceiling lead me to suspect the same architect for the tunnels as for my basement flat: Chez Mercedes and Cyril on Rue Gower, Saint Jean, Terre-Neuve.

I follow her conversation to the entrance then up the stairs. Her stride is long, like her legs. Her jeans are snug on her wide hips and tucked into her knee-high leather boots. Her woollen sweater has a geometric pattern like on the sweater Mercedes is knitting for Cyril. She reminds me of a girlfriend I had in England. I only ever had one girlfriend besides Elsa. She was tall like Norah, confident, leading the way, always smiling. We lived together for five years until she decided I didn't talk enough, didn't spend enough, didn't work out enough, didn't joke enough.

Two of the library staff go by while we wait in line to be served. I wave and smile. They don't wave in return. "What if they never find the book? What will you do then?"

"If they don't find the book? Let me see." She pauses. "I'm too old for a tantrum, too gourmand for a hunger strike, too conservative to protest. I suppose I'll settle for a request to interlibrary loans. Is that a double espresso? The English aren't a nation of espresso drinkers, are they?"

Even in Norway, where I hardly spoke the language, no one ever singled me out. They didn't say, "Who's your family?" or "Where do you belong?" I know they think I'm slow when I don't respond to their questions: "How ya doin?" or "Where ya been?" or "How ya getting on?" I've made a list of them. Somehow, they never sound right when I say them.

"I'm an Englishman with espresso genes."

We find a place for two between tables crowded with students, backpacks and laptops. She throws her sweater over her chair. Her t-shirt shows a seal with a speech bubble: *Have cod, will travel.* When I ask her what it means, she launches into a spiel about how the scientists at Fisheries and Oceans aren't doing enough to protect the fish and how the Greenpeace protestors are corrupting the facts. "You obviously haven't been here long," she says.

"Obviously. And you?"

"I'm from the bay. A place called Cliffhead."

"Population?"

"At last census, there was one goat, three sheep, two horses, seven – or is it six – chickens, three dogs and me."

"Is it a farm or a zoo?"

"It's a point of land near Cape Spear," she says. "Twenty

minutes from St. John's in good weather, no traffic."

"Main attractions?"

"A pond with rowboat, the highest meadow, widest view, when the fog isn't around, and the greatest attraction…" She pauses. "My book collection."

"History books?"

"Lewis Carroll, mostly… as in Alice-Mad-Hatter-White-Rabbit-Tweedledee-and-Tweddledum-Jabberwocky-Cheshire-Cat-through-the-looking-glass-down-the-rabbit-hole-in-Wonderland Carroll. Two thousand five hundred thirty-four volumes plus two patients at the book hospital. That's a small collection. Smallwood, our provincial premier, had 18,000 in his library. Judge Furlong's library…" She gives me a mini history of libraries in Newfoundland.

"Are you a historian or a librarian?"

"I could use a librarian's skills for managing my collection. I'd like to create a catalogue so I can compare features, document how the editions differ."

I explain, probably in too much detail, how she could create a searchable digital catalogue. "I'll get you a copy of the software."

"I wouldn't know where to start. Nor would my computer. What are your rates like?"

I laugh. "Exorbitant but I have a special promotion on now. Free lesson."

"You need to see the collection first. Cliffhead is not that far from town. Do you know the route to Cape Spear?"

So far I've only dared explore the distance between campus and my flat. Henry took me to Signal Hill the first week I arrived. The panoramic view was hidden in the fog. Henry watched the couple necking in the car parked beside us. "He'll be sliding his hands up her sweater any minute," he said. They noticed him, scowled then drove off. We sat in his car with the engine purring, the heater on tropical and the radio humming in the background while we watched seagulls pluck leftover French fries from fast-food containers in the parking lot trash bin.

"Why don't you send me the directions by email." I take my card from my wallet and hand it to her.

She checks her watch then stands. "I've got to head to a meeting," she says. "I'm glad I ran into you."

"I'll order tea next time, fit in with the ex-pats, be more British."

"Don't be more of anything," she says. She grabs her bag and reaches over to touch the side of my head. "Take care of the bump." She nudges around the table then slips into the crowd of students.

I stare ahead with the cup hugged between my hands. Someone moves, unblocks my view and I see him for an instant. It's not hard to miss his bald pink head. A student moves, blocks the view, and I can't see him anymore. When the student moves again, Francis is gone. I crumple my cup then toss it on target into the waste basket, my most successful accomplishment for the day. Students shuffle off to class; the space clears. I catch a glimpse of blue through the window. The curtain of fog has lifted to reveal a city behind it.

The change reminds me of a fable about two brothers. They begin their day as usual, starving. That night, they profit from confusion over a dog's name, Estula, which also means *are you there?* to steal cabbage and a lamb from a rich and stupid neighbour. Moral of the fable: he who laughs in the morning, cries at night. What is sadness and despair at night, is happiness in the morning.

CHAPTER SIXTEEN

quarto, folio and octavo

NORAH EMAILS DIRECTIONS: *DRIVE TO the end of the harbour front, past the railway station, take the first set of lights left up the hill past the whale mural, then follow the signs for Cape Spear.* What's the end or what's the beginning of the harbour front? Signs for Cape Spear? What signs? I backtrack to the other end, drive past a train station without trains, turn left at the light then head uphill by the whaling wall. *After about 5km, you'll see a road heading to the ocean.* Five kilometres from the lights? From the end of the harbour? From the start of the mural? Details are important.

The first road leads me to a metal graveyard with mangled carcasses of rusted car wrecks stripped clean to the chassis. *You'll come to a concrete post with a sign saying: Cliffhead private road.* I back up, wonder if I have a spare tire then swing left onto the next road that points to the coast. Private road? More like a private path with private potholes, bordered by stunted, private vegetation. I manoeuvre a sharp private turn, dodge private ditches filled with runoff from the public rain of the night until

I reach a clearing where I see three buildings that make me think of windmills without the mills or lighthouses without lights.

I park next to another car. Three large dogs race towards me barking. Norah calls to them and they go to her side. She holds the collars of the two biggest dogs, one in each hand. The third beast poses at her side, looking like a butler or an official greeter. "Welcome to Cliffhead," she says as I climb out of my car. "Say hello to Octavo, his brother Quarto, sister Folio, the runt of the litter. One black, one yellow, one chocolate, colour-coordinated Labrador retrievers. Gently guys. Octavo. Be nice, Octavo! Bad dog, Octavo! Heel, Octavo!"

Dogs with names of book folds poke their noses between my legs, circle me then dart off after each other. The smallest hangs behind to sniff my boots.

Norah turns to face the building behind her. "I promised you it was a magical place. Ever seen a hexagonally shaped building?"

"Never even imagined it."

Her hair is tied into a ponytail which makes her face more visible. Her freckles overlap on her cheeks near her nose. "You have to think snowflakes, honeycombs, crystals," she says.

"Red snowflakes?"

"The red one, the smallest of the three, is for storage. It's not mine. We call it the Crimson Hexagon. Next to where you parked is the barn. The bigger one straight ahead is where I live. My horse Biblio is grazing in a meadow behind that grove of spruce trees. I don't give names to anything I eat. Here we have three sheep, a goat, a few chickens and too many fleas to count. That's it for the intros."

I tag along after her up the slope to her house. In the other direction the path leads to a rocky beach. The goat glares at me. I try not to picture it at the end of a fork and knife.

An Imperfect Librarian

We crowd into a porch filled with firewood, outdoor clothes, rain gear and dog gear. From the porch we walk into a kitchen with wooden floors and ceilings. We go round the table in the middle then into a living room with an area rug, two wooden rocking chairs and a worn, blue couch with a patchwork quilt thrown over the back. We stand in front of floor-to-ceiling windows. She points to Signal Hill and Freshwater Bay, then in the other direction to England. Sunlight filters through the fog. I watch its shadow moving in the beam on the floor.

"Depending on the wind and the light, the water can look green, blue, grey, black, white, silver or any combination of those," she says. "Very rarely, it's smooth as glass. More often, the wind is savage and the waves are wild. This place sets more records for extremes of weather than any other place on earth."

"I've been reading about the weather lately. Foggiest, windiest, coldest."

"For Cliffhead, add wildest, fiercest, moodiest, and then, when we least expect it, the finest."

She leads me through a French door to a study with wall-to-wall bookshelves that reach to the ceiling and a desk at the centre.

"I feel like I'm inside a book."

She shows me a first edition of Carroll's *Alice in Wonderland*. "It's insured for twelve thousand dollars. Nobody touches it unless their hands are clean as a surgeon's."

"I don't suppose you lend them out?"

"You might as well ask a parent: 'Do you lend your children?'"

I follow her back to the kitchen then to the living room. The stairway is so steep I'd call it a ladder. The top floor is a bedroom and sitting room combined.

"Welcome to the peak," she says.

QUARTO, FOLIO AND OCTAVO

It reminds me of a wooden tepee. Six beams rise from the floor and join at the top. I tilt my head to look out through the windows.

"At night, with the lights off, you can lie in bed, gaze at the stars, constellations and the moon through the skylights. I call them star-lights. Sometimes I can see satellites."

Her bed is a double mattress on the floor with a puffy duvet and more pillows than I want to count.

"Most nights, regardless of the weather, I leave the windows open while I sleep so I can hear the waves. When the winds are right, I can hear the foghorn."

When I lie in bed and gaze up at the ceiling pipes, there are no stars or satellites visible. There's a housefly that flits from corner to corner. I've watched him so much, I can almost predict his moves. As far as sounds go, there's the occasional trickling of water through the pipes and Cyril's snoring from the living room above.

We gaze at the sky through the star-lights. A patch of blue appears from out of the fog.

"Congratulations! You brought the fine weather," she says. "Just in time for our hike."

CHAPTER SEVENTEEN

birds on crutches

ONE OF HER DOGS BOLTS past and knocks me over into the bushes. I climb to my feet, brush off my clothes, then another races by and nearly drives me into the branches of a tree. Norah waits at the crest of the hill. "We're heading to Gull Pond, property of Ray Harding," she says. "He had it stocked with trout a couple of years ago. People have been poaching from it ever since. He posted a no-trespassing sign but that didn't stop them. Then someone convinced him that the poachers were actually the gulls, so now he sets traps for them on top of three- and four-foot poles around the pond. Most often, it's other birds or small animals like squirrels that get trapped." She turns her head to the side so I can hear her talk while she walks. "I found a dead crow in the traps once. Another time, a kingfisher. I put it in a box in the barn, gave it food and water. It died in two days."

I follow close behind then stop to catch my breath. "What did you do then?"

She turns round to wait for me. "Held a wake, invited his

buddies. Drank like fish, they did. Next day, everyone flocked to the funeral. Cremation, of course. I sprinkled the ashes over the pond, remained in control of my emotions during the ceremony, fought off the memories kind of thing." She winks, smiles then goes on ahead of me again.

I try to keep up. The last time I went hiking was in the Pyrenees during an elementary school trip. My energy levels were higher then. The terrain wasn't as unpredictable, nor as steep. Every so often I glance over my shoulder in case the dogs are behind me. When the trail levels off, I shorten the distance between us.

"The bushes lining this part of the trail are blueberry," she says, talking over her shoulder again. "Up at the pond, you'll see marshberry bushes. I picked so many berries last year, my fingers were black for the season."

I stop and rest my hands on my knees to catch my breath. "I've never picked berries."

She stands next to me. "When the season comes I'll give you lessons if you want. Like with blueberries, I'll teach you not to pick the red ones, because they're green."

"I'm lost already."

"In Newfoundland, green is a synonym for unripe. You'll catch on."

"People keep telling me that."

She lays her hands on her hips then looks up into the trees. "Listen. It's a white-throated sparrow." She sings. "Oh sweet Canada, Canada, Canada." The birds are quiet. The dogs run past again. Norah runs after them. "See you on ahead," she says. "Take your time."

A branch from the side of the trail makes a good walking cane. Long legs make it easier for stepping over small boulders. While I walk, I stare down at the rocks, the moss, the dark brown powdery soil and the roots of trees that surface, sinewy

An Imperfect Librarian

like veins in an old hand. The dogs run up behind me. I can almost hear the screeching of their paws when they stop suddenly then backtrack to sniff my cane. One of them clamps its teeth around it.

"Stop that now. Immediately. I said stop it. Did you hear me?" We play a tug of war. I make a quick pull. The stick hits a rock and cracks in two. The dog bolts to the side then runs off. I run to catch up with Norah. "Sorry, did you say something?" I ask her.

She's sitting on a boulder waiting for me. "I was talking to myself. Ever hear of *Fahrenheit 451*. Destruction of books by fire?"

"Every librarian knows it."

She doesn't leave me time to catch my breath. She hops off the boulder. This time, she walks slowly but turns her head to the side so I can hear her. "I liked the idea of people memorizing books to save them from the book burners. That's where I got the idea. When I'm on the trails, I practice reciting portions of Carroll's work that I've memorized. It takes my mind off the climb. Your *Fahrenheit 451* choice?"

When I was a boy, Tatie told me fables and tales at bedtime. I'd fall asleep dreaming about powerful barons tricked by helpless peasants, mean husbands punished by spiteful wives or fools made wiser by encounters with tricksters. "*Fables and Tales of the Middle Ages.* Probably not great literature but they entertained me when I was a boy. They started as oral stories so it makes sense to learn them by heart."

"In the middle ages," she says, "people had better memories for stories. They had databases for brains."

"I use databases every day at work."

She stops then turns round. The top buttons on her shirt are undone. Her chest is shiny with sweat. "And when you're not working?"

"I only arrived at the end of last summer. Haven't got my bearings yet."

"You're one degree closer to the equator than Paris is and 3.5 hours west of Greenwich. The .5 entitles us to our own time zone."

"You're a geographer and a historian."

"A wannabe meteorologist, a wannabe librarian, a wannabe biologist, a wannabe writer. I dibble and dabble."

"Like a Renaissance woman?"

"Renaissance women aren't known for their rubber boots, knapsacks or Labrador retrievers. Come on guys," she shouts to the dogs. The smallest one, Folio, runs up to us then hops on me with muddy paws. "Down, Folio!" Norah says. I take off my boot to see what's digging into my heel. Norah eyes the blister. "We'll have to ship you off to the pre-amputee ward where you'll be kept company by the half-legged birds on crutches."

I put on my boot just as the other two dogs appear. Eventually, the hills give way to a slope, then to a plateau. The reliable terrain of the trail gives way to more unpredictable wet patches. We reach a fork. Norah points into the distance. "There's a tiny stretch of sand around that corner and a rowboat. I'll be gone for about a half-hour while I check on Ray's traps. Water that cold has restorative powers. Maybe you can restore your foot to its pre-blister stage."

CHAPTER EIGHTEEN

row, row, row your boat

IT'S NOT AN ALUMINIUM OR fibreglass rowboat; it can't hold more than two people at one time; it hasn't seen a paintbrush since it was first constructed; and it's probably not engineered, like modern vessels, for energy efficiency, but it's an ideal place to rest after a hike. It's lying part in the pond, part on the strip of shore. It doesn't rock when I climb in with the extra weight of my naked blister. I sit then lie across the centre seat with my hands clasped behind my head and my legs dangling over the side. I tease the water first with the tip of my toes, then submerge my feet all the way to the ankle.

Strips of fog float past, thin as sheets of onion paper. My feet feel numb in the glacial water but the rest of me is warm under the sun. The songbirds signal back and forth. I count the syllables, note the pattern of the long *Oh sweet* followed by three quick *Canadas*. Norah said it's a natural waltz rhythm. I remember when she put her hand on my waist then bent over to tighten her boot. I could see her breasts, plump like the top of a loaf of bread. I lie under the sun in the boat and think about squeezing breasts, resting my head on breasts, poking my face between breasts, bouncing breasts, pressing up against breasts with my chest or–

There's a sound of someone or something moving through the bushes. I pull my soggy feet in from the water. They throb from the cold. A black dog like Norah's retriever leaps over the bushes towards me. He does a flip-flop on his first attempt to hop into the boat. I roll up the legs of my trousers, hold onto the side then lower one leg at a time into the water. The boggy bottom feels like partially melted ice cream.

A voice yells, "Raven! Raven!" The baseball hat appears first, then the red-and-black chequered jacket, then the rubber boots. The dog is standing on the shore barking at me. "Raven!" the man orders. "Come here." The dog doesn't respond. He eyes me like there is a steak hanging over my head.

"Hello. Nice day. Those are my boots there on the shore. Would you mind passing them here?"

The man walks over to them, picks one up then throws it into the water next to me. I let go of the boat to shield myself from the splash.

"Raven!" he shouts. "Get it boy! Go on! Get the boot."

It's floating away in the ripple created when it hit the water. My arms aren't long enough to hold onto both so I let go of the boat and grab the boot just before the dog does. I teeter for an instant then catch hold of the boat again.

"Get it, Raven! Get it!" the man cries.

Raven makes it to shore faster than I do. He jumps up at the boot. I hold it over my head.

"That's it," the man says. "Go as fast as you can."

The soft bog of the pond was easier on my feet than the sharp rocks on the shore. I can't go fast. Not without something on my feet. "I wasn't fishing if that's what you think."

"Fishing?" he shouts behind me. "You better not be after

my trout. I stocked this pond five years ago. They're worth money now."

Once I have the two boots, I don't stop to put them on my feet. I step away from the shore onto a grassier area. "I wouldn't even know what a trout looks like, let alone go fishing for it." I look over my shoulder. "Why did you throw my boot in the water?"

He's following me. "Trespassers deserves what they gets."

I pick up a stick off the path and hold it in the air. The dog notices instantly. I throw it as hard as I can in the direction opposite where I'm heading. Raven turns around and runs after it. Ray chases after him. Once they're out of sight, I put on one boot. It weighs a few pounds heavier. What's the point of paying more for waterproof boots if they're only waterproof from the outside? The blister's so big, it would need a boot of its own, so I go barefoot on one side and cradle the boot close to my chest.

Norah joins me on the trail not long after. She surveys me top to bottom. "I thought you were going to soak your heel."

I give her the opposite of an abridged version of events.

"I'll run to the barn to get the horses. Won't take me long," she says.

I've never been on a horse before but she's already well into the curves of the trail with the dogs in obedient pursuit before I can say no. I don't want to stay where I am because I might run into Ray and Raven. Regardless of where I go, it won't be fast, not with a wet boot, sock on one foot, and nothing more than a blister on the other. There's a detour that leads to a meadow. It's not where Norah went but it's grassy instead of rocky and muddy.

I sit on the ground with my back against a boulder like I'm in a front row seat in an open-air theatre. I dig into my pockets for the complimentary trail-mix bar they dropped in the shopping bag when I bought the boots that gave me the complimentary trail blister. The foil wrapping has kept it dry but hasn't improved its taste. One bite and I throw what's left into the meadow. I poke the wrapper into my pocket. I watch the gulls cross above then below the horizon as if it was a rope tugged tightly at either end. A piece of an iceberg bobs around in the waves not far from shore. The scene reminds me I should trade my binoculars for a camera.

Elsa kept our camera, her camera, the one I gave her for Christmas three years ago. She took nice pictures of her yoga teacher in his poses at the gym, in the hot tub at his house, in his living room. The landscape pictures she brought back from her trip to India with him were colourful. She caught on to photography quickly. She was right when she said her yoga teacher was far more photogenic. I'd never look like him no matter how many weights I lifted or how many pretzel poses I distorted myself into.

I'm not in the meadow for long before a bank of fog creeps around the point and smothers everything in its path, including the sun. I roll over onto my knees then to my feet. A beady-eyed, bushy-tailed fox bolts to the side, just as startled as I am. His front paw is mangled as if he'd chewed it off. The foghorn blows and he darts off on three legs with the trail-mix bar hanging from his mouth. I hop up onto my feet while I lean onto the boulder for support. The horn blows again. I cut a path through the grass in the thick fog. It doesn't lead me where I expected. I remember Cyril's story about the man in Gros Morne park. He separated from the others to follow a side trail then the weather turned stormy. "The crows got him picked to the bone by now," Cyril said.

Dogs bark.

"Here. I'm hererererere." I shout until my breath expires while I'm hopping towards the barking. Something cuts into my blister. The dogs bark again. "I'm hererererere." I stop suddenly like I've hit a wall. The wall is a beast as big as a moose. The moose is wearing a saddle. Its reins are held by a man with a head of red hair that would make a fox jealous. We stare at each other.

"You scared me. I thought for a second it was a moose. I'm Carl. You must be with Norah."

His forehead buckles when he squints at my feet, at my face, at my clothes then at my feet again. I realize I've left my other boot at the foot of the boulder. "Did you see the fox with the injured paw?" I ask. "Got caught in one of Ray Harding's traps, I suppose."

He tightens the saddle on the horse then watches the dogs chasing the scent of the fox in the meadow. When Norah arrives, she introduces us from on top of her horse. "Walter will help you mount," she says. "Other foot, Carl. Give him a boost, Walter. Hang onto the horn, Carl."

He's smaller than me but much stronger. He nearly catapults me over the top to the other side. He adjusts the stirrups. I haven't yet steadied myself in my seat when he gathers the reins, shifts the horse to face the other direction then leads us down the trail. Most of the time, I can't see anything because I have to duck to avoid boughs hitting me in the face. The swaying makes me nauseated. For a while, when I was a young boy, I wanted to be a cowboy when I grew up. "You'd be no good at it," Papa told me. He was right.

CHAPTER NINETEEN

partridgeberry cognac

I MAKE USE OF HER SHOWER to clean up before we eat. Her bathroom reminds me I should be searching for a new flat – one with a reliable shower where the water doesn't decide to change temperature when you're covered in soap. Most mornings, the hot water is cold because either the dishwasher or clothes washer is running or someone is in the upstairs shower. There's a portable heater in my bathroom. I used it once. The power went out in the entire house.

After the shower, I join her in the kitchen. The wood floor feels warm under my feet. "Here's some wine to kindle your insides," she says. "The arctic char is in the oven: no goat meat tonight. If I'd known you were going to be in the pond, I would have asked you to fetch trout for supper."

"How about some fox meat?" I tell her about the fox in the meadow.

She opens the oven, then reaches inside. "The foxes are harmless."

"That's more than I can say for Ray Harding."

She lays a hot platter on top of the stove then takes off her oven mitts. "I'll have a talk with him. I'm sure if he sees you there again, he'll treat you like one of the neighbours."

"Is Walter your neighbour?"

"Walter lives next door in our old house. We moved there from the south coast when I was a teenager. Originally, he was one of my father's pupils. He took care of my grandmother and then my father until he died. He helps me around the property, ploughing my road in the winter, cutting hay in the fall, preparing the garden in the spring."

"Has your father been dead long?"

She passes me two six-sided plates and two six-sided glasses for water. "Help me set the table. I'll tell you about him while we eat."

She's the third person besides Edith or Mercedes and Cyril to invite me for a meal. I've had every type of delicacy including figgy duff, bakeapple bunts, caribou stir-fry, stuffed moose heart, fish and brewis, and barbequed cod tongues. This is my first arctic char in phyllo pastry with a partridgeberry-cognac sauce. We sit at the table. Steam rises off the fish. While I was in the shower, she changed into a sleeveless t-shirt with track pants. She's not wearing a–

"If my father was here," she says, "you'd see the biggest man with the smallest voice, the most exhausted eyes from reading all the time, the most passionate intellect. Talk about superlatives. Reading was a religion to him, something he worshipped and proselytized about." She serves me then runs back and forth to the fridge or cupboard for things she forgot to put on the table.

"When you meet someone new for the first time, you'll typically ask: 'Where are you from?' or 'What do you do?' William, Will for short, would ask, 'What are you reading now?' So, Carl, what are you reading?"

"*Robinson Crusoe.*"

She holds up her glass of wine like she's toasting. "Will would have approved. He would have quoted from it or launched into a lecture on first-person narratives. You'd wonder if you were sitting in an English class listening to an absent-minded professor."

It's not easy to eat with the dogs staring at me through the glass door in the porch, drooling for table scraps. "He would have made a good librarian."

"Libraries weren't common in outport Newfoundland, especially in the small communities where Will and his mother lived."

"A bibliophile with no books?"

"He had books. Only a few at first, thousands eventually. His mother, Esther, was a midwife."

"She gave birth to books?"

She pours more wine. "You could say that. The island's birth rate was one of the highest in the world back then. Esther travelled on coastal boats to communities where her services were needed. Will was always in tow. Most of the time, they paid her in-kind with firewood, plenty of eggs, vegetables, game, fish. Sometimes, in exchange for a service, she'd ask for a book or two. That's how Will became a collector."

"Is your mother still living?"

She gets up from the table then goes to the porch to let the dogs outside. A draft of cold air flows into the room. She sits at the table again. "Will didn't really want children, not after spending so much time with a midwife. That's why he married my mother. She was a widow, ten years older. She couldn't have children, or so they thought. She passed away when I was young. He brought a copy of *Alice's Adventures in Wonderland* to the hospital. Baptism by books. Before I turned seven, I had over six hundred."

"You're like Matilda in Roald Dahl's book. She read all of Dickens before she turned five."

"I can't claim the same, although I did have the largest collection of children's books in any outport, probably on the whole island. It earned me more suspicion than friends though. I would have been more popular with the largest marble or doll collection."

"I remember a boy in school who brought a collection of objects his father, a doctor, removed from windpipes, ears and nostrils. Stuff like popcorn, peanuts or peas."

"English peas?"

"French."

"Is your father a doctor?" she asks.

"A civil servant."

"Retired?"

"Retired to be a curmudgeon."

"Your mother?"

"She retired to Spain once my umbilical cord was cut. We haven't been in touch since."

"I can see the Spanish in you. If you'd come to St. John's thirty years ago you would have been mistaken for a sailor. You have an exotic look for around here."

"Please don't remind me."

swindled share of summer

AFTER THE MEAL, WHILE NORAH putters in the kitchen, I browse her collection. I count twenty-four editions of *Alice's Adventures in Wonderland* and as many or more of *Through the Looking Glass*. The two framed photos on the wall are more interesting to admire than count. There's one colour photo of what looks like Norah with Will and her mother. The other is a black and white photo of a fair-haired boy with Will. When Norah enters the study, I shift my attention back to the books. She takes me on tour. She hands me books to examine as if they were fine jewellery. She explains the differences between editions, which ones are most sought after and why. "Am I going into too much detail?" she asks.

When the tour ends, I help her carry in firewood from the outside to the porch. After, we sit in rocking chairs by the floor-to-ceiling window. She talks about her collection and favourite passages in *Alice in Wonderland*. I tell her a story I once read about a Mr. Benjamin Button who was born old then grew younger as he aged. She asks me about my work and then about my parents.

"No mother? What about your mother country?" she asks.

"Nowhere, really."

"It's settled. You'll become a Newfoundlander. Our population is declining. We can always use a few more people here."

"For ballast?"

"You're funny," she says.

"I don't look like a Newfoundlander. I certainly don't sound like one. I wasn't born here."

"Being a Newfoundlander is not about being born here. It's about how you connect with the place. It's about missing the island when you go away, putting up with the fog, walking face-first into gusts, that sort of thing."

"My friend Mercedes says there's no bad weather only bad clothes."

"The weather here isn't the scoundrel people make it out to be. Besides, there's so much else that makes up for it. You don't mind putting up with someone who makes your life more difficult if they have finer qualities to compensate. We may not have the weather but we have other things."

"Like char in phyllo pastry?"

"That's a Cliffhead specialty. Like people who surprise you and come through for you. Years ago, before I lived at Cliffhead, I went camping up the flats of a river with a friend. There were sandbars and grassy islands everywhere so we assumed it was fine. That night it poured out of the heavens. Daylight came, we packed up. We had to wade in water up to our knees, carrying our gear until we made it to the road, then to our car. In that short distance, one person shouted, 'Do you want a cup of tea?' Someone else called out, 'Do you need a place to stay?' Not everyone is so welcoming. You met Ray Harding so you know that. But he's the exception."

"You may not have the weather but you have Ray."

"You'll get used to the weather after a few winters. You'll accept your swindled share of summer because you'll have that bond with the place."

"Cyril, Mercedes' husband, says it comes only about once every two or three years."

"Well, it's coming this year for sure. And it's going to make up for the winter."

"Sounds like an apology."

"A request for forgiveness. If the good weather continues, we'll have one of the best summers on record."

"Best by Newfoundland standards."

"Best standards there are. How many other islands can boast their own dictionary, encyclopaedia, dog and pony?"

"Or hexagons, Ray Hardings, three-pawed foxes, birds on crutches?"

She laughs, lays down her glass then runs her fingers through her hair. She stares out the window into the darkness. "Once you've been this close to the ocean, you'll never want to live anywhere else. We call it the sea. Ever hear the folk song?" She sings while she taps the one-two-three rhythm on the arm of her rocking chair. "The sea, the sea, the wonderful sea. Long may she roam between nation and me. And everyone here should go down on one knee. Thank God we're surrounded by water."

I applaud.

"Once you have its salt flowing in your veins, you're never the same," she says. She closes her eyes and hums to the music.

I close mine. Before long, the rocking makes me sleepy. I stand then go to the kitchen. "I've had more fresh air in the last five or six hours than I've had in years. I'm going to 'give 'er,' as they say here."

"Giver?"

"Cyril's been giving me lessons in local sayings. I'm sure he told me that give 'er as in 'give it to her' means speed on, go on or to go."

"I hope your friend isn't charging you too much for those lessons. You can't use give 'er in that sense. You can say, 'I'm going to take off' or 'I'm going to hit the road' or 'burn some rubber' but not give 'er. Anyway, it wouldn't sound right coming out of you."

"I told you I could never be a Newfoundlander."

"It's not about the accent." She pours the last of the wine. "We should meet again, share stories, music," she says. "Who knows? By that time, you might have learned your book of fables off by heart."

"If you don't mind waiting years."

"I was thinking of this coming Saturday."

"Fine, as long as you don't expect me to have it memorized by then. I have a busy week ahead." I open the porch door. The dogs get up off their beds. Three tails wag and swat each other.

Norah squeezes in past me, opens the door and they rush outside. "I know the perfect place," she says. "I'll send you an email with the information. In the meantime, what about your lost boot? I'd lend you one of mine but I doubt it would fit." She laughs. "I'd say that fox is wearing your boot over his wounded paw. He's strutting around with the new prosthesis, showing off to everyone."

I step outside. "They were too tight. I was thinking of returning them to the shop."

"You could still try," she says. "Sorry. I bought a pair of boots here. I'd like to return one. Can I have half my money back?" She calls to me as I limp to my car. "Watch out for the moose and the foxes, especially the ones with boots. They're fast."

The road is dark until I reach Shea Heights and look out onto the glimmering lights of the city. I negotiate the curves down the steep hill. Maybe the eight hundred dollar brake job was a fair deal. "Deflated, impotent, prick of a car." I pass the mural of the whales, the *Welcome to the Waterford Valley* sign, the Railway Museum, drive across the harbour-front with the crab vessels, the rusted Russian trawler, the offshore supply vessel and the *Arctic Explorer*, up Prescott Street where the muffler probably wakes people from deep sleep. "Worse pain in the arse than a severe case of haemorrhoids."

The flat is dark and damp. No woodstove here. No view of the ocean. No peak with star-lights. No wooden floors or bookshelves with single volumes worth more than I'll probably ever have in my bank account at any one time. The spider in the corner has trapped two more earwigs. Let that be a lesson to them. It's about time the extended family of earwigs moved out. I open the fridge for something to do. The container of beef stew is still there. Mercedes made it fresh for me two weeks ago. After four days in a row of beef stew, I've lost my appetite for it. It's too watery for the trash bin. I can't flush it down the toilet because the last time I did something like that, the toilet clogged up then overflowed. I was forced to ask Cyril to come down, everything was floating around on the bathroom floor and I thought I could never feel so embarrassed.

I crawl under the blankets with my clothes on. It's too cold to take them off yet. I'll wait until I'm warmer and hope I don't fall asleep before then. I reach for the *Robinson Crusoe* sticking out from under my mattress. I stay with him until my eyes are too tired to focus anymore. By then, he'd been living on the island for four years or long enough to stop regretting his fate:

> *I could hardly have named a place in the uninhabited part of the world where I could have been cast more to my advantage.*

CHAPTER TWENTY-ONE

the apocalypse of the book

HENRY AND I SIT IDLY like spectators at intermission for some sports event except that our intermission *is* the main event. In the Room below, they're trying to wake a man who's asleep in a chair. Henry shifts his attention like someone channel surfing. "Behold the geometry on her. Where's the binoculars, Carl?"

"I brought them to the flat." They catch my eye. They're on top of my filing cabinet behind him.

Henry notices instantly. When I make a move to reach them before he does, I trigger a painful muscle spasm in my leg. I don't know if it was the hiking or the horseback ride but I can barely move. "We're not using those anymore," I tell him.

He takes them from the cabinet then puts them to his eyes with his glasses resting on top. He focuses on me. "Don't go saying there are no binoculars when they're glaring directly at you. Lying is a despicable, dirty act. If you'd been raised a Catholic, you'd know that." He laughs then shifts his view from me to the window. He sits with them glued to his face. "You'd be better off wasting your time with a woman like her instead of one who's mixed up with Francis," he says.

I reach across to take them from him "You don't know that for certain. Anyway, I spent one day with her. Give me those binoculars." The muscle contracts and I gasp with the pain.

He leans away from me. "Francis and Myrick are a duo, a pair, a two-some."

"How do you know?"

"Because I keep my eyes and ears open and my prick pointed, unlike some people around here," he says.

"I tried dealing with Francis. I asked for his inventory. He told me–"

Henry lays the binoculars on the floor under his chair. "You're wasting your time with inventories. What library really keeps an accurate account of which books they have? The proof's with Blumberg. He stole twenty million dollars worth. After they caught him and found the loot, most of the titles had to be auctioned off. The libraries didn't know they'd lost them. You're the one who fancies numbers. Imagine how many books go missing that we don't even know about. Imagine the books that are never requested, never borrowed. That's the majority of our collection. If someone can devise a scheme to steal the books, most of the time, no one will ever notice anything's been stolen. If a man eats a can of beans, does he know which one caused the fart?" Henry lays his empty cup on my desk, picks up the binoculars from the floor then puts them in front of his eyes again. "The view is grand today."

"You're doing that to irritate me because you know I can't move."

"Don't be assuming you're the focus of my behaviours," he says. "You're not that fascinating."

"If I was after twenty million dollars, I'd rob a bank instead of a library."

"That's because you have no imagination," he says. "Bibliophiles are driven by passion, not profit. Theft is merely interlibrary loan for them. They want to free the books and give them the attention they deserve."

"It's still stealing."

He lays the binoculars in his lap then takes a handkerchief from his pocket to wipe his forehead. "Think of all the lonely books on the shelves accumulating dust, growing old and frail. Can you blame a lover of books for wanting to bring them home where they'll be appreciated?"

"Borrow them. That's what a library is designed for."

"As the anonymous Arabic proverb so wisely observes: 'He who lends a book is an idiot. He who returns the book is more of an idiot.'"

"What about he who steals a book?"

"Depends whether he has the luck and smarts to get away with it."

Henry stands then puts the binoculars back on the cabinet. He walks over to the window for a last inspection and turns to face me before he goes to the door. "They'll replace all books with computers one of these days," he says with a resigned tone. He raises his right hand in the air and stares up at it. "Instead of the sound of pages turning, you'll hear the staccato of fingers plucking keyboards." He drops the right hand then raises the left. "Instead of the seductive aroma of aged paper and leather bindings, you'll be nauseated by the stench of burning dust from overheated circuitry."

Next, he holds both hands waist height, palms up, in supplication. "Instead of brilliant minds engaged in reading books so thick they need to rest on a table, you'll see light-headed drones flitting through electronic pages with as much depth as a television commercial." With both hands raised and his head bowed between them, he adds, for the finale, "Language will be eroded, knowledge will be reduced to bits of information pulsing through wires, contact will be limited to an electronic signal, while the book…" Here, he pauses, raises his chin to gaze out onto an invisible audience then drops his hands to his side, palms facing out. "The book is abandoned, unattended like an ancient relic gathering centuries of dust."

"Bravo, Henry. See you tomorrow," I add as the curtain closes on another wasted afternoon.

CHAPTER TWENTY-TWO

seagulls' dreams

MY ONLY SUIT SHARES CLOSET space with a mop and broom, four shirts and a variety of cleaning fluids. My Hawaiian shirt has mould growing on the palm trees. There is one advantage to living in the basement: I can call on my landlords for advice at any time. I merely go up the stairs, open the door and yell. "Cyril? Mercedes? Hello. It's me." Cyril is an electrical inspector. When I first moved in, he gave me a tour of the house to show me the rewiring job. He described the codes, explained the circuit box in detail, opened a few outlets and led me outside to see the connection to the street pole.

"How do I look, Cyril? I'm going out to dinner tonight. The pants stretched since I wore them last. Shirt's a bit wrinkled, isn't it?"

"You're asking the wrong person. Mercedes!" he hollers.

I follow him into the kitchen. He tells me about his plans to start up his own business. "Do-it-yourself appliance repairs. Call Cyril for help repairing your own toasters, washers, dryers, VCRs. I'll charge by the minute."

Mercedes appears from upstairs. "Hello stranger. Sit down and have a snack."

I work my way through a bowl of pea soup and a homemade roll while Cyril pokes at a toaster and Mercedes tidies the kitchen. They're both always busy at something. If Mercedes is forced to sit, she knits. The vacuum gets so much use, I'm surprised it's still running. I butter my roll. Mercedes is wiping out the fridge and Cyril has his nose in the toaster. A spark and smoke shoot out of it. Mercedes shrieks like she's seen a mouse. Cyril laughs. I clean the ashes from the spark off the butter on my roll. Mercedes throws her cloth at him. "Will you take that contraption off the table while Carl is here."

"Jesus, maid. If you'd stop making me do chores for you night and day, day and night, repair the toaster, finish the clapboard, put out the garbage, shovel the snow, rake the leaves, fix the sink, I'd be out building the shed. In no time, I'd have my own workshop. You wouldn't have to complain anymore. Isn't that right, Carl?"

I don't know anything about electricity between wires or spouses. I eat my roll and say nothing. Mercedes opens the oven then sprays something inside. "I'm leaving that to soak," she says. "Don't go closing the oven door, either one of you."

Cyril jabs at the toaster. The kitchen smells of burnt toast, smoke and whatever Mercedes sprayed on the oven. I start on the tea with a date square. They're not coffee drinkers. Mercedes starts on me with her usual questions and comments, punctuated with the name Nancy. I tell them about the highlights of the visit to Cliffhead: the dogs, the hexagons, my boot, the trail, the rowboat, the blister, the fox, the horses, the char, partridgeberry-cognac sauce and, finally, the lights of the city on the drive to town.

Cyril twitches his head to the side like I've seen some men

do since I came to Newfoundland. "Yes, b'y. Give 'er," he says.

Mercedes thinks my shirt is too wrinkled and my trousers are too big. "You can't go on a date looking like a streel," she says. "If you were with Nancy, you'd have all your shirts ironed."

Cyril twitches his head again. I imitate. He laughs. "You'll get it right one of these days. Don't give up."

After my snack, Mercedes irons my shirt and Cyril lends me a belt. One side of the buckle imitates a plug, the other a socket. I don't have far to walk to the restaurant because it's only at the bottom of Cathedral Street. *Watch for the mermaid*, Norah wrote in her email. It would have been hard to miss the statue or sign: *St. John's Mermaid, Bar and Restaurant*. The inside is an imitation of the interior of a seventeenth-century ship. The waiters are dressed as sea captains and pirates. The waitresses' legs are wrapped in sparkling mermaid tails. Norah is ordering a drink as I arrive. She introduces me to a couple she knows from the trail association. There's the usual "Where do you belong? How long you here for?" Then, the mermaid interrupts: "Ready to go to the main deck?" she says.

Norah smiles at me. We follow the mermaid along a corridor bordered by canvas sails. The main deck looks authentic except that it's filled with tables and chairs in addition to barrels, cannons, rigging, ropes and a ship's wheel. Our wooden table has a clear glass-top finish. In the centre there's an oil lamp. We study the menu in a dim light. I settle on Corte-Real's Bacalhau. Norah doesn't like salt-cod dishes so she takes a Captain Eastwood's peppered halibut steak. She orders a bottle of wine that costs more than both our dishes combined.

Elsa rarely drank wine because she was afraid it might interfere with her performance as a runner. Meat interfered with her yoga so we hardly ever ate that at the flat or when we went out. Any form of fast food was out of the question. I only ever ate hamburgers or French fries when she wasn't around.

"Are you athletic?" I ask Norah when we begin eating.

"Chopping wood, cutting hay, shovelling horse dung or snow, chasing chickens or the dogs, digging in my garden, grooming the trails – I guess you could call that athletic. At Cliffhead, every season has its..."

While we eat, I try to listen to her description of life at Cliffhead. The couple at a nearby table distracts me. I can't see the woman's face but from behind she has the same style blond hair as Elsa.

Norah continues to talk while the mermaid tops up her wine glass. "If they'd stop giving me new courses every semester I'd have time to do the chores and..."

On the far side of the room, people sing happy birthday as a mermaid walks into the room carrying a cake with sparklers on top.

"...he thinks he can make me teach in an area I'm not qualified for. I told him I didn't know anything about Canadian history. It's not my area. 'We didn't hire you to teach Newfoundland history,' he said. I said, 'Well you...'"

I remember when Elsa and I blew the last of our English pounds on an expensive restaurant for our final meal before we moved to Norway. We talked about where we'd live and whether, one day, we'd be able to afford a house. Elsa said she'd only buy a house together if we were married.

The couple at the other table hold hands. The mermaid brings their bill. They pay then prepare to leave.

Norah talks while the mermaid takes our plates away. "I've been to the union, the dean, the VP. They were as bad as he was. If they don't give me tenure, I'll..."

The woman at the other table stands then turns around. She doesn't look anything like Elsa. But maybe Elsa is different now. I haven't seen her since I moved to Newfoundland over seven months ago. I like to remember how she looked when we married. Tatie called her *La Princesse de Carl*. Papa approved highly of our marriage. Elsa was Norwegian. The Normans are a tribe originally from Norway, he told me. I was marrying a descendant of a forceful breed of warriors. Bravo, son! Bravo! he congratulated me.

We don't bother with dessert or coffee. The mermaid brings our bill.

"Ron Hynes and his band are playing at the bar," Norah says. "He's great to dance to. He wrote 'Sonny's Dream.' I should have played it for you while you were at my place. That's an excuse for you to come back." She smiles then lays her hand on the side of my head.

We walk from the restaurant to the bar. Before we're there, it starts to pour. The water brings out a strange smell off my clothes. I remember that I need to find a place to live where my trousers and shirts don't have to share closet space with cleaning fluids.

"Howdy. Five bucks cover," the woman at the door says.

There are no seats but we find a place to stand not far from the musicians. They're set up on a stage that's barely a foot off the floor. The music starts. I ask Norah if she'd like a drink. She says something but I can't hear her because we're standing near the speakers. I reach my ear closer to her mouth.

"I said I love that song!"

"Would you like to–" I wasn't going to say dance but Norah throws her jacket onto the back of someone's chair, grabs my hand and leads me out onto an empty floor in front of the band. We have plenty of room since no one else is dancing. Norah needs the space for when she twirls with her arms spread out. I try to stay facing her. It's not easy because she turns often. I'm relieved when the song ends.

"Let's have a hand for the first dancers of the evening."

Norah claps while I take off my jacket. She grabs hold of my hand again. The band starts another song. In no time, the dancers have gone from two to twenty. Someone moves a table to make more dancing space. A dancer bumps against me from behind and pushes me into Norah. She rests her hands on my shoulders. I lay my hands on her waist. When the music stops, she lets go.

"I'll get you a drink–" I'm about to say of *water* but the man on stage with the cowboy hat and guitar interrupts.

"We're gonna give our dancers a chance to slow down, maybe do some huggin'. Don't get carried away." The audience laughs. "In a world of romance don't miss out on the chance to be dancin' the 'St. John's Waltz,'" he sings. The audience applauds.

The music starts and more bodies squeeze onto the dance floor. "You lead," she says.

I take hold of her outstretched arm then reach my hand around her back to draw her close to me. I move with the flow of all the other bodies. I close my eyes while the man with the cowboy hat sings about seagulls dreaming seagulls' dreams. The song ends. We clap and the music starts again. I stay with her on the dance floor until she tells me she needs to pee.

"If you go to the bar, I'll have a double Morgan and coke, single ice," she says. It takes me two songs to get served. When I come back, I see she's found another partner. I leave her drink on the edge of the speakers near where she's dancing. Now and then, her arms fly up in the air and sway. The band plays another song, then another.

"Time for a break," the cowboy finally says. The audience groans. "Right after this song." People applaud. "We had a request from…" He pauses while he talks to someone on the dance floor. "We're gonna play a request from Norah. This is 'Atlantic Blue.' If you can't be with the one you love then you know what you gotta do."

Norah waves for me to join her. I squeeze a path through the dancers. "Where've you been?" she says. She rests her head against my chest and hugs her arms around my waist again.

"Are you OK?" I ask.

She doesn't say anything but she holds me tighter. I reach my arms down over her back. Her shirt feels damp. The dance floor is so crowded we can barely move. The cowboy closes his eyes while he picks his guitar and sings about haunted dreams, whispered names and vacant hearts. She doesn't move except to follow my steps. When the song ends, she raises her head off my chest and stares up at me. "Can we go?" she says.

I wipe a strand of hair out of her eyes. "You can't drive."

She kisses my neck. "Take me home? Stay with me?"

I pull her close and bend down to kiss her head.

That night, after a calm ride under a clearing sky and waxing moon, I visit her shower for the second time. We blanket our bodies in soap then waltz in the shower. From the bathroom, we head to the top floor of her house where the six sides meet and where the heat from the woodstove hides from the drafts.

She's already downstairs when I wake in the morning. She serves me homemade bread with local butter and her marshberry jam. After breakfast, we go to the cove below her house where we throw sticks into the waves. The dogs fight with each other to retrieve them. We compete to see who can skim rocks the farthest. She drops two miniature beach rocks into my pocket. "Hold onto these. When you put your hands in your pocket, rub them between your fingers, close your eyes then imagine you're here in the cove, at Cliffhead, with me."

CHAPTER TWENTY-THREE

i read, therefore, i am

"**W**HAT HAVE YOU GOT TO be so happy about?" Henry says.

"Must be the weather."

"Are you mad? The rain is coming down horizontal. What were you doing this weekend?"

"Same old thing."

"Not out at Blackhead with that Reading Room woman, were you? I hope not."

"It's Cliffhead and her name is Norah Myrick."

"I called you but there was no answer," he says. "I wanted to know if you'd chauffeur me around while I scouted for space to rent for my bookstore."

"You can't retire for another four years. Why are you looking for space now?"

"There's no harm in being prepared. Who knows? I might open it before I retire. There's a space on Duckworth Street that would serve the purpose. Fabulous view of The Narrows. I might put a coffee shop in the back after a few years. I'll have the finest bookstore in eastern Canada, maybe anywhere in the country. Why settle for anything less than the best, right, Carl?"

"I have just the title."

"Allow me to guess," he says. "Bits and Bytes Books?"

"Not quite. Ever hear of William Buggage, Bookseller?"

"Name doesn't mean anything to me."

"Finally, I found something you don't know."

"You're allowed one tidbit of information more than me," he says. "There wouldn't be a measure of my own greatness without a relative indication of the degree of your intelligence and knowledge."

"William Buggage: Rare Books, Charing Cross Road. He's a character in one of Roald Dahl's short stories called 'The Bookseller.' Buggage scans the papers daily for death announcements of wealthy gentlemen. He cross-references with the *Who's Who*. From there, he picks a widow to defraud for some of the late husband's money. His assistant, Miss Tottle, prepares letters for the widows to offer condolences and to demand thousands of pounds for outstanding book purchases supposedly made by the late husband: *Why Teenage Girls Prefer Older Men* or *How To Please Young Girls When You Are Over Sixty*."

"I must pick up a copy of that last one for myself," says Henry.

"Without exception, the widows always pay up. Then, one day, something unexpected occurs. A Mrs. Somebody, I forget the name, it doesn't matter, arrives in the shop with her son and two other men. Buggage has made a mistake by sending her a letter. It's simply not believable that her husband could have purchased those volumes. Tottle and Buggage launch into their adopted roles. They lecture her about how men will be men and there's no harm in it. Then, the widow asks if the books were in Braille. Tottle and Buggage have no reply. The other two men are from Scotland Yard."

"The moral of your story?" Henry says.

"You could call the shop Tottle and Buggage: Booksellers. I always thought that would be a brilliant name for a book shop."

"Took you long enough to make your point. I've already chosen the name: The Crimson Hexagon. There'll be no other bookstore of its stature and quality in the country, perhaps across the entire continent. You never know, if business is swift, I might be needing an assistant such as yourself."

"There's a Crimson Hexagon on Norah Myrick's property."

"We'll have to keep an eye on this woman, won't we?" says Henry.

"Only a few minutes ago, you were warning me not to have anything to do with her. Now, you're telling me the opposite. Then I suppose you'll accuse me of being confused."

"I'll take no responsibility. Anyone who knows you is well aware of your ability to fog things up on the finest of days."

"Who cares about a Crimson Hexagon anyway?"

"According to the writer Borges, it contains all-powerful, magical books."

"Sorry, Henry. You've lost me. I don't have your imagination. My native blood is Cartesian, you know."

He raises a handkerchief to his forehead. "Cartesian? You? What's your motto? *I don't think much, therefore I might not be much?*" He laughs. "Dust off your imagination, take it out of the closet, allow it to see some light for a change."

"I'll put it on my priority list."

"Write at the top: find out about that hexagon and stop sitting around drinking coffee and staring down into Room."

"You did tell me not to get mixed up with her. You may not remember–"

An Imperfect Librarian

"There's a difference between watch her and latch onto her. One's a w and–"

"I get it, Henry. No need to explain."

He rises up from his chair then heads towards the door.

"Before I forget, a quick question for you. I'm conducting an informal poll. You know *Fahrenheit 451*, right?"

"The destruction of collective awareness by the book burners. Author Ray Bradbury. Classification: dystopic science fiction. Appeared in serial form in *Playboy* magazine, later published by Ballantine Books, 1953. What about it?"

"If I responded with that much detail you'd say I was boring."

"You are boring," he says.

"Supposing you were in a *Fahrenheit 451* situation and you could save only one book to memorize, what would it be?"

"That's easy. *The Joy of Sex*."

CHAPTER TWENTY-FOUR

culinary mutiny

ALWAYS AT 3:45, ALWAYS IN the same reading carrel, always out of the line-of-sight of the cameras. I visit the carrel where she used to sit. I turn my back to it the same way Francis did when I was watching him through the binoculars. One of the surveillance cameras points to the counter, the other at the front door, the final one at the other end of the Room. I show the clerk the notes from a scrap of paper in my pocket: *Mainwaring, H.: Collected papers.*

"That's archival material," he says. "I can get it for you but you have to sit at the table there. Material that old has a line-of-sight restriction on it. Oh yeah, and there's also a glove restriction."

"You must have it mixed up with something else. I saw a woman borrow the same thing not long ago. She took it to that carrel over there in the corner. I work here. I'm Head of Digital Library Systems."

"The rules are the same for everyone. Doesn't matter if you're a head of lettuce, that material has a bunch of restrictions on it. Do you still want the gloves?"

"It was you. I remember now. You're the one who served her. You let me look at her request slip."

"You're that bibliosomething guy."

"Yes. You gave the woman a file that she looked at there in the corner carrel. It's the same one you're telling me is restricted."

"I don't make the rules."

"I know. I'm asking why have the rules changed?"

"You'll have to talk to Francis Hickey about that. Do you want me to see if he's around?"

"I'll wear the gloves. Forget it."

He disappears into a room behind the counter. A woman walks up to the counter. I move out of her way. The clerk returns with a folder. He lays it on a desk while he answers the woman's questions. Finally, a man appears from behind the counter and asks if he can help me.

"I'm waiting on the folder there on the table."

He passes it to me and I sign the slip on top. He brings me to a table behind the counter. The white gloves remind me that my hands are much longer than most people's. The disorganized pile of letters, maps, illustrations, diary entries and ship logs remind me that I'm not really sure what I'm looking for. Now and then, I stop to read transcribed pieces like the diary entry from 387 years ago to the month.

April 21, 1613

Today we executed two atrocious villains for sodomy and another six for mutiny. Yet another 8 were given 70 lashes each. During the executions, the First Lieutenant concerted with the crew in argument against me for acquittal due to want of evidence. This traitorous behaviour won him favour from the men.

Likewise, it made more ardent their disaffection towards me and gave them further pretence to mutiny. I sought no redress nor did I make him answer for his seditious conduct and for his design to place my authority at hazard. Newfoundland remains 5 or 6 days out of reach. The winds and current conspire against progress towards land. My brain takes fire at the worry of the schemes against me.

After more than an hour of sorting, I still don't know what I'm searching for. I hand the material to the clerk. He writes something on my request slip. Before I go back upstairs, I make a detour past Francis' office. His door is ajar. I saunter by, knock, wait, knock, then poke my head inside. I see it right away on the shelf near the door – the same photo at Norah's house. Will and a young boy – Francis and Will. There's another photo of Francis, smiling, with his arm around Norah. I move towards it for a closer look.

"You don't give up do you, Brunet?" his voice says from behind me.

"It's not what you think. I wanted to talk to you about Special Collections inventories. Your door was open."

He's not smiling. "I've already explained about my inventories. I thought you would have remembered our meeting on the stairs–"

"Eventually, you'll have to give me access whether you want to or not, Francis. Things are changing around here and it's for the good." I edge my way out through of the door.

"Listen, Brunet. Let me give you some advice. Just because you have an accent and a PhD doesn't make you welcome around here. On the contrary. Now get the fuck out of my office." He starts closing the door before I'm even all the way out. The sign reads: *Francis Hickey, Special Collections Head.* I'm tempted to cross off *Head* and put *Ass* in its place, but the hall's surveillance cameras would never let me get away with it.

When I tell Henry about the incident, he replies with his usual "I told you so." I shouldn't have said anything about the photos in Francis' office. That only gives Henry ideas. "There's a cook at the Faculty Club who moonlights in security and surveillance," he says. "Put him on Francis' scent. Find out what he's up to after hours."

"Maybe I could convince the cook to poison him," I propose.

"Wouldn't bode well for his career as a cook. I have a better idea. Why don't you have him keep one eye on that Reading Room woman at the same time?"

"You mean Norah?"

"I mean the woman I hope you're not shagging round with. The woman in the photo with Francis. The woman whose father was caught stealing. The woman you saw stealing in the Reading Room. Do you need me to read you the textbook on this, Carl, or are you waiting on the footnotes?"

CHAPTER TWENTY-FIVE

blowed up and pickled

ERCEDES AND CYRIL INVITE ME for supper to celebrate my first summer in Newfoundland. On the menu is jigg's dinner with a side plate of flipper pie and fresh greens. I have no idea what I'm eating but they're so enthusiastic I can't refuse. "It'll give you a powerful spring cleaning," Cyril proclaims.

Mercedes describes it as a tonic. "There's more fortifying iron in that meat than in any other." It's Cyril's dogberry wine that's fortifying. The more I drink, the more I can tolerate the taste of the flipper pie.

Cyril asks his usual questions about the flat to make sure the sink hasn't clogged up again, that the leak from the pipe in the ceiling is under control and that the pesticide worked against the carpenters and earwigs. Mercedes wants to know if I'm still willing to consider nurse Nancy as a potential date. "You should see her new hair style. She had it straightened and gold streaks added. If I looked that gorgeous I wouldn't have to be with the likes of Cyril. Don't mind me. Cyril knows I'm only joking with him."

"She's wrong there, Carl. The women are always after me. I had to marry Mercedes to stop them chasing me."

"Nancy mentioned something about being invited to a wedding this summer," Mercedes says. "Second weekend in August. Are you available? She's dying about your accent."

My summer plans don't include anybody by the name of Nancy. Ray Harding is going to Alberta to work for the summer. He's offered Norah use of the pond and rowboat in exchange for checking on his house. I promised to lend her a hand with the chores and help with her catalogue. In exchange, she's teaching me to swim and to row.

"I'm not free in August but I know someone who is. Remember my friend Henry? Works at the library with me? He has a much better accent than mine. It's Irish. Nancy will love that right away."

"Anyone but an Italian," Mercedes says. "She went out with a tile layer a couple of years ago. He finished every floor in her house in ceramic. When she broke it off, he hung on like he was grouted to her."

"I know the feeling. Henry wouldn't behave like that though. He's always accusing me of being too sentimental."

"Women love sentimental men," Mercedes says.

"Depends on the woman, I guess. I'm sure Nancy will find him attractive if she gets to know him. He can be coarse on the outside but he's a marshmallow underneath."

"Enough about Henry. What about this one Norah? Who's her family?"

"Her father's dead, but I know plenty about him. There's a family friend, Walter. I haven't actually spoken to him. He doesn't talk much to anyone, apparently. There's Ray, her neighbour. I sort of know him. We don't get along. Norah and I have only known each other a short while. I haven't met her friends yet. She hasn't met you either."

"Invite her over any time," Mercedes says.

"I'd rather wait till I find my own place. I love the flat, I mean the apartment, but I might need something larger soon, like a home of my own."

Mercedes and Cyril know when I come in, go out, flush the toilet, do laundry, shower, go to bed and wake up. Likewise, I know if they're arguing or in amorous agreement, cooking or cleaning, watching the news or a movie. Sometimes, I wear earplugs. I forgot to take them out once when I went to the office. It's tempting to leave them in. Libraries are much quieter than most places but noise becomes more conspicuous – like Cyril's snoring when there are no competing sounds.

"What do you need to go moving for? I've been living a quarter of the century with the wife and the daughter. It's good to have another man around."

"By and by, Carl will be wanting a place of his own and a woman of his own," Mercedes adds. "You know what they say: A woman is to the hearth what blood is to the heart."

"Or maybe it's a woman is to the heart what water is to a live wire."

"What does that mean, Cyril? You'll have him confused with that talk."

"You don't need to be an electrician to understand my meaning. You only need to be a man, right, Carl?"

"For now, I'm not thinking about a woman for the hearth or the heart. I simply want to enjoy my first summer on the island."

Cyril piles more food on my plate. "You'll be blowed up like a harbour tomcod," he says to me. I hold out my glass for a refill of the wine. Blowed up and pickled. Must be all the salt beef in the jigg's dinner.

An Imperfect Librarian

CHAPTER TWENTY-SIX

a comfortable silence

THE KING E. LIBRARY GOES into hibernation for July and August. Edith and Henry leave for summer vacation. The Reading Room might as well have white sheets thrown over the furniture. Henry will be relieved to know he didn't miss anything important. Work is tolerable because the library is air-conditioned. If it wasn't, I'd fall asleep at my desk reading reports about information system design. There's no time for reading reports on weekends at Cliffhead. We finish painting the rowboat after we plant her garden and before we tackle the job of widening the trail beyond the meadow. The garden fence needs to be repaired to keep out the lettuce-loving animals. The soil needs more lime. We build a sifter out of leftover chicken wire and some boards to remove the large stones. I shovel. Norah sifts through the soil. I promise to help with her catalogue on rainy days but there are none.

I borrow a library book on astronomy to guide our sky gazing. We don't use it much because we're too exhausted for anything but sleep by the time we're in the peak of the house. We take advantage of the long days to be outside until nine or ten o'clock. The dogs wake us in the morning not long after the sun comes up. We spend the day at the cove, meadow, pond, around the garden, in the woods or by the barn. The first thing we do when we come inside is take a shower together to wash away the sweat, smoke and salt from our skin. It's the best part of the day – worth getting dirty for.

Norah doesn't invite me to Cliffhead on weekdays. The routine is Friday to Sunday night then back to work Monday morning. I don't usually visit without letting her know I'm coming. This time is different because it's her birthday. She kept it a secret but the database didn't.

The morning drags on. Not long after lunch, I stop by the flower shop to pick up the roses. The florist piles them into my arms. "Sixteen red, sixteen yellow, sixteen pink. Lucky woman," she says.

"Lucky man, you mean."

She stares at me. "Sorry. I assumed–"

"No, you're right. I mean I'm a lucky man."

She smiles.

I visit the delicatessen for picnic food, the liquor store for champagne, the ice cream shop for a cake engineered to stay frozen up to two hours out of the freezer. I roll down the car windows, turn the stereo on high and head to Cliffhead with the warm wind blowing in through the open windows.

I pull up to my usual spot by the barn. That fact that his vintage Jaguar is parked there makes it less usual. I leave the birthday celebration in the back seat. The dogs are nowhere in sight, the house is locked, the barn empty, the cove deserted. I run up the trail towards the meadow in my office clothes during one of the hottest days on record, dodging the roots and rocks under my feet, almost falling, almost suffocating. Two or three times, I stop to bend over. I rest my hands on my knees and wait till my heartbeat slows down.

I take a shortcut through bushes and trees that scratch at my face and neck. I scramble through the thickets, push branches out of my path and hop over muddy puddles. The pond is calm, rowing conditions ideal. The three dogs are swimming after the boat. He's wearing a hat over his bald head, She's wearing her hair down. He rows smoothly and quickly. The dogs will soon pick up my scent if they don't drown before they reach the shore. I take the same route back, not as fast, not with the same lightness. I drive directly to my basement flat. It's cool enough in there to keep a cake frozen and roses fresh. That might be useful if I hadn't thrown the lot in the garbage when I stopped for petrol.

"How was your week?" I ask her two days later.

"The usual. Pass me an extra garbage bag, please."

I'm helping her gather fly-ridden, part-rotted, salt-baked strips of seaweed to use as garden fertilizer. The dogs poke their noses in the slime left on the beach rock when I peel off a layer of seaweed.

"I meant to ask you about the photos in your study. Who's the boy with the light hair, the one your father has his arm around?"

"The photo on the shelf with my father and the boy?" Norah says. "Francis Hickey. He was one of my father's pupils."

"Like Walter?"

"Yes. Except that Will preferred Francis over Walter, over all the boys, over his own daughter. No matter what Francis did, he did it better than anyone else. My father loved him. He left his entire collection to Francis, including the Crimson Hexagon."

"That was generous of him."

"Will suffered a lot in the years before he died. His diabetes was out of control. His mind and eyesight were failing. If it wasn't for Francis and Walter, I don't know what I would have done. Walter read to him. Francis worked on his collection, listing everything, annotating the items."

I sit next to her on a piece of driftwood. "Why was your father collecting this material in the first place?"

"Because that's what you do when you're a collector. There's an incredible excitement always pushing you to reach the boundary of the collection. Often it's infinite or unattainable. That's what makes it frustrating and compelling at the same time. It's something to be passionate about."

"Or obsessive."

"It's no different than someone who decides he's going to scale a high mountain. He does that, then he sees a higher mountain and he puts all his energy into reaching the top of it. Then he sees another one and so on and so on. That was Will. It made for a difficult life. But that's the price you pay when you're really passionate about something And the collecting was only a small part of it. He had to organize, catalogue and transcribe most of it. The originals had to be preserved. If that wasn't enough, then he had to write about it in his book, *The Emerging Voice of Newfoundland*. Another time, it was *A History of Reading and Writing in Early Newfoundland*. The title changed every week."

"Were you collecting along with him?"

"Not while he was alive. Will, Walter and Francis had their no-girls-allowed club. Reminds me of the History Department. I don't want to think about that. It's too depressing. Come on!" She pulls me to my feet then drags me towards the waves.

"Stop. It's too cold. We'll get wet," I tell her.

I reach my arms around her back and legs to try to lift her in the air. I lose my balance then stumble onto the rocks, laughing. She takes off her shoes and socks. I do the same. We roll up the legs of our trousers then wade in the water holding hands. It's painfully cold. I jump back out and pull her with me.

"Come on," she says. "You'll get used to it."

We walk from one end of the cove to the other in water up past our calves then past our knees. Later, before the daylight blue surrenders to black, we sit on a piece of board washed up on the beach in the yellow glow of the bonfire with the smell of seaweed on our hands and smoke on our clothes. Sparks shoot out. The heat is intense. The backs of the minke whales rise and fall not far from shore. The gulls dive then swoop up with fish tails hanging from their beaks. Behind us, way up on top of the cliff, her house watches over us. The fire crackles and pops. We stare into it with no more than a comfortable silence between us.

CHAPTER TWENTY-SEVEN

berry-picking lessons cont'd

NORAH MAKES A CONFIDENT BET that she can teach me to swim by the end of the summer. I'm confident she'll lose her bet. "Swimming is natural: like making love," she says.

I've had six weeks of lessons and I've swallowed as many litres of pond water. Even the dogs are laughing at me behind my back. I'd be better off in a swimming pool or in any water where there's an actual bottom. I don't care if it's concrete, sandy or rocky. Anything but boggy. It would also help if Folio would go with the other dogs instead of swimming around me. Norah says Labrador retrievers make the best seeing-eye and water-rescue dogs. I wonder what that says about me.

She coaches me from the shore. "Hold your head above the water."

I practice gripping the boulder with only one hand. "Are you talking to me or Folio?" My feet touch the bog – or is it something furry rotting at the bottom? A carcass of a moose floated to the surface in June. Norah said the people from Wildlife took it away. How do they know there isn't a second or a third carcass? I could be floating in a graveyard for moose. I kick my legs while I hold on with one hand. Norah is laughing.

"This is entertain–" I mean to say, *This is entertainment for you, isn't it?* I swallow water on *tain* then cough up the other words. I move to the shallow side where I can touch the boggy bottom. "Rather have my head underwater than my feet in this guck," I shout.

She wraps her arms around her knees and hugs them to her chest. The straw hat hides her face from the sun and from my view. "There are some pockets of quicksand. Not too many. You should be safe," she says.

I run out of the water. Folio swims like mad to keep up with me. I grab a towel then wrap it around my waist. "What's so funny?" I ask.

She rummages through the backpack of supplies then pulls out a bottle of wine and uncorks it. "Nothing," she says. She holds out a glass to me. "Glass of wine? Some cheese and bread?"

I shake my head and finish drying off. "Do I have anything to do with nothing?"

"I was laughing because you believed me. There's no quicksand, Carl."

"I knew that. I was worried about the sharks."

She takes a gulp of wine then gapes at me. "Are you serious?"

"See? You're as gullible as I am." I put on my shoes then go to the bushes for a pee. When I come back, I watch Folio chasing after flies near the edge of the water. I lie on the blanket and reach out my hand to rest it on Norah's back. The strip of sand bordered by bushes and shrubs is barely wide enough for

BERRY-PICKING LESSONS CONT'D

the two of us. "Do you ever come here with Francis?"

She doesn't say anything. She shifts forward so that my hand is no longer on her back.

"I was just wondering, since he was such a close friend of the family."

She lays an empty glass in the sand, lies back on the blanket and covers her face with her hat. "I don't want to talk for now. I'm taking my siesta."

The clouds move in to give us shade. I turn on my side to face her. I trace an imaginary line along her warm, smooth legs then run my hand up the inside of her thigh. I slide my hand under her swimsuit and squeeze her breast. She turns to face me. While we kiss, she pulls down the straps of her suit over her chest, hips, knees then feet. I pull her naked body against me.

Folio disappears in search of shade or because she doesn't want to listen to the heavy breathing. She reappears later when we're lying quietly on the blanket. The lop on the pond hitting off the rowboat is the only sound. Norah lies with an arm and leg stretched across my body.

Folio drops a wet tennis ball near my face. I raise my head off the blanket and throw it into the pond. She darts off then comes back in an instant and shakes water over us. Norah squeals and sits up on the blanket.

We put on our clothes and pack up our supplies. I throw Folio's ball in the boat and she jumps in after it. Norah pushes off then joins me on the centre seat. I row with one oar. She rows with the other. The breeze is shy so we make good progress with little effort. Folio sits in the front to scout for birds. We round the point and watch for the shallow spots where hidden boulders might scrape off the bottom of the boat. When we're almost to the beaver's house, we stop to rest. Norah splashes water over her face then flicks some at me. Folio barks and the boat tips to the side.

"That's enough," she says. "Let's go to the beaver's house."

The mound of grey sticks and mud is larger up close than from the other end of the small pond. Norah holds the oars while I move up front next to Folio so I can grab hold of a boulder. "There's no smoke coming out of the chimney. There mustn't be anyone home."

She lays the oars in the spine of the boat and throws the anchor overboard. "Don't be silly," she says. "It's too warm for a fire today."

We change places. She climbs out of the boat onto a boulder near the shore then dives into the water. Folio bites at the drops that fly into the boat. I count the seconds, wondering how long someone can hold their breath. I lean over one side but I don't see her. I lean over the other and there's still no sign. I can't save her if I don't know how to swim. I lean over the other side again. There's a splash followed by her laugh. She climbs back onto the boulder then into the boat.

"You're a naughty, mischievous girl," I tell her.

"Bold, saucy, a know-it-all and whatever else you want me to be."

I wrap a towel over her shoulders. The boat rocks. "Do you think it's a good idea to be drinking and swimming under water?"

"Don't be on my case, please. Did you see the beaver?"

I lean forward to kiss her. "No beavers, only a siren who rose from the depths to nearly capsize the boat."

She rubs her head with the towel to dry her hair. "Beavers can be troublesome. They chop down trees, divert rivers, pollute the water. You don't want to get giardia."

I run my fingers along the contours of her face. "Common symptoms?"

"Growing a big fat tail."

BERRY-PICKING LESSONS CONT'D

135

"Like a siren?"

"Like a beaver," she says.

"How do you think I'd look with a tail?"

"Wouldn't match the life jacket. Aren't you hot sitting in the boat with that thing wrapped around you?"

"That thing will save me from drowning."

She runs her fingers through her hair like a comb. "Not if you only wear it in a boat or on land. Test it in the water, why don't you?"

I climb out onto the boulder while I listen to her reminders about three-point contact. "Hang onto the rock with one hand and the boat with the other while you step out," she says.

The water may be cold but at least I don't have to touch off the bottom. It's a bog-saving vest as well. I kick and wave my arms to warm up. I play with the buoyancy and swirl round. I turn to face the boat. She's drawn the anchor and she's rowing away from me.

"Where are you going?"

"Swim to me," she calls.

I wave to her. "Come back! I can't swim. I can only tread."

She's not waiting for me. "You're swimming now."

The boat leaves a smooth wake behind it. I shatter it when I thrash my arms and kick my legs. That's the closest I'll come to swimming. I stop partway to hold my breath and dip my head under. There's not much to see in the murky waters but then something moves. It could be a terrified trout, an eel or the carcass of a moose thawing out. I kick and thrash then kick and thrash some more. I reach the shore as she's anchoring the boat.

She hands me a towel. "Hurray for you! You officially swam the length of the pond."

I wipe my face. "That wasn't a very nice trick to play on me."

She kisses my shoulder. "Forgive me. I'll make up for it. Anything you want."

An Imperfect Librarian

"What about if you answered my questions about you know who."

"Who?" she says.

"There you go again. I told you, you were evasive about him."

"Not Francis. Please. We're having a great day. Don't spoil it again."

"Again? Since when did I spoil the day? I just swam the length of the pond? What else—"

"I didn't mean today. I mean in general. Enough about Francis."

"You make it sound like that's all I ever talk about."

"Sometimes it feels that way, yes."

"Feels to me like you're avoiding the topic."

"Not paranoid by any chance are you?"

"That's not a very nice thing to say."

She stands. "I didn't say you were."

I grab her hand. "Stay here with me. Don't go. You can make up for forcing me to swim across the pond if you bake me one of those blueberry pies you've been boasting about."

"Blueberry pie it is, once the berries ripen and you help me pick them."

She sits on the blanket. I put my arm around her. "But not the red ones because they're green, right?"

"I told you you'd catch on," she says. "Next, you'll have to learn about the berry grounds, berry pots, berry notes, berry ocky, berry duffs and berry bank."

"Is that it?"

"Nowhere near. You still have to learn how to tell marshberries from partridgeberries, which berries to pick before the frost and which after. There's the whole issue of knowing where to find them. One year, there might be thousands in an area. The next year…"

BERRY-PICKING LESSONS CONT'D

Norah talks as she lies down and rests her head in my lap. She knows how much I like to run my hands through her hair. I close my eyes and remember a day at the shore with Papa. It was the summer before we moved to France from Quebec. We had to get up while it was still dark. I felt sick sitting in the back seat during the long drive. A man and woman came with us. The man took us to a park in the forest with a lake. He lent me his fishing rod. When I caught a fish, Papa shouted, Bravo. He hugged me. I wrapped my arms around his neck and he hugged me even tighter. Later, we had a picnic on the shore. After supper, I lay with my head in his lap while he talked to the man. Papa rested his hand on my head. I closed my eyes, but not because I wanted to hurry things.

CHAPTER TWENTY-EIGHT

newfoundland style

THE BEACH IN THE COVE is a noisy place, especially when the tide is high. It wouldn't be nearly as noisy if it were sandy. I could get used to the quick splashing sound of waves hitting the shore. It's the rocks smacking off each other like firecrackers when the water recedes that I can't ignore. Sometimes, I'd like to be able to flick a switch, turn off the noise and enjoy the calm of the cove. The stream is noisy but I don't mind the predictable sound of its flow. It barely whispers when it gushes over, under and around the rocks into the ocean.

There's no shortage of comfortable rocks to sit on while I read, watch the whales chasing the capelin, the gulls hovering over the whales, or the dogs chasing after the gulls. To the left is Europe. To the right is the community of Blackhead with its fourteen houses, church no bigger than a house, and corner store where I go to buy milk when we run out. They also sell souvenirs including pink poodles made of nylon and homemade soaps and salts with names like Partridgeberry Punch, Iceberg Explosion or Spruce Sizzle.

I visit the store for the first time one Saturday afternoon in August. Norah is baking a cake. She runs out of baking powder so I offer to fetch some. She gives me directions and I find it without any trouble. I pull up in front of the one-storey building with its yellow clapboard and red door. It's no bigger than a garage. The hand-painted sign says *Oliver's*. Two girls are sitting on the store's steps sucking on orange popsicles. They follow me inside. The bell tinkles when I open the door. The girls seem to like that so they open and close it until the woman behind the counter shouts for them to give it up. "Sorry, Mrs. Oliver," they respond in unison with their matching orange lips and moustaches.

The inside is nothing more than an oversized closet stacked to the ceiling with supplies. I ask if they have baking powder. Mrs. Oliver seems surprised, almost affronted at the question as if I'd made inquiries too personal. "My darling," she says, "we got that and everything else besides." She rhymes off a line of products from baking soda and baking salts to baking flour. I say the powder's fine for my purposes and she says what purposes would those be and I say someone's baking a cake and she says now who might that be and the conversation goes in the direction it always does. "How long are you here for?"

I know exactly what she means, unfortunately. Long enough to buy the powder, I reply. Is that so, darling, she says and I ask how much and she wants to know if I'll be paying in Canadian dollars and I tell her of course and she says special price for strangers and I say not necessary and she says don't be talkin'. She places the tin of powder in a paper bag. "Anything else for you now? Some homemade bread, homemade fudge, spruce beer? Salt beef's on special this week."

"Another time, maybe."

"Special's over tomorrow."

The bell rings again when I walk out the door carrying two

five-gallon buckets of salt beef. The girls with orange popsicle lips follow me outside. I turn the car's ignition over and over. A loud squeak from the engine startles the girls. They shriek then laugh. Mrs. Oliver comes outside. A man calls something to me and I roll down the window.

"I said you won't be doin' much drag racin' with the likes of that jalopy."

The audience swells to a couple of teenage boys wearing baseball hats and jeans so low you'd think they had no bums. A frail man with grey whiskers lays down his empty wheelbarrow to watch the scene. He takes off his khaki hat to wipe his brow with the back of his hand. Four eager dogs show up, tails wagging and tongues hanging.

"How much do I owe you?" I say to the man after he diagnoses the problem and gives the battery a boost.

"Go on wit' ya," he laughs. The others look at each other and laugh with him. "We're all neighbours round here."

I reach my hand out the window to give a final wave before I head onto the main road. They watch me so closely you'd swear it was the departure of a loved one heading off on a perilous journey. By the time I'm back at Cliffhead, Norah has given up on the cake. Just as well. The best-before date on the powder says it expired three years ago. The house is too warm for baking anyway.

We stuff supplies into our backpacks then head to the cove for the afternoon. I'll need physiotherapy on my shoulder from throwing sticks into the water for the dogs. "That's enough. Go lie down," I order them. I take my seat on a flat rock in the stream then dabble my feet in the water. Norah spreads the blanket just under the cliff in a thin band of shade. She sleeps for a while. I don't sleep, not sitting on a rock in the stream, not with the three dogs splashing about, dropping sticks at my feet, in my lap, or worse, on top of my book.

NEWFOUNDLAND STYLE

Later in the afternoon, Norah goes to the house to fetch the lobsters while I build the fire. When the water in the pot is boiling, we drop the creatures in. I think I hear them squeal but Norah says it's not possible because they have no voice boxes. By the time we finish eating, the coals are giving off so much heat we have to move farther from the fire. The orange glow is hypnotizing. The dogs claim Norah's blanket for their siesta. The sun is low in the sky and soft on the eyes. Norah rinses her hands in a bath-size pool in the stream while I stoke the bonfire.

"It's so warm. Come see," she calls. She strips down to her bra and underpants.

I throw another piece of driftwood on the fire. "Does the sunburn hurt?"

"Not while I'm soaking in the salt water," she says. "Join me?"

I strip down to the evidence of my own time in the sun then sit beside her in a pool like a lukewarm bath. The rock underneath is smooth. I lie back on my elbows, almost completely immersed in the water. She turns onto her stomach then leans forwards to kiss me. I balance on one arm and reach the other around to draw her closer. All of a sudden, a cold wave splashes into the pool. Norah jerks forwards. I lose my balance and fall backwards. The salt water pours up my nostrils. The wave is sucked back out and I sit up, coughing. Norah laughs.

"What's so funny this time? I thought I was drowning."

"That's your christening," she says. "You now have the salt of Newfoundland flowing in your veins."

"I'm relieved to know I got something out of it."

"Let's go back to the house, take up where we left off," she says.

"Make love Newfoundland style?"

"Whatever style turns you on."

An Imperfect Librarian

Later, under her star-lights, under her blankets, under the weight of her body, with skin that tastes of salt and smells of smoke and without the worry of a mischievous wave, we consume each other.

CHAPTER TWENTY-NINE

an edible apology

RAY HARDING RETURNS FROM ALBERTA at the end of August. He's fuming that we painted the inside of his rowboat the tricolour pink, white and green of the Newfoundland flag. We avoid the pond to spend our time nearer the hexagons or the cove. The delivery of birch and spruce needs to be stacked into cords. The bakeapples then the blueberries ripen. We travel into the back-country to pick them. On more than one berry-picking expedition, we cross paths with hoards of flies. Norah told me their names – nippers, stouts, garnippers, gallynippers, black flies, sand flies and horse flies. She forgot to mention the flies that are drawn like vampires to the fresh blood of strangers.

Classes begin, students crawl out of the woodwork, the library comes alive again. Edith's telephone number appears on my caller ID daily. Her emails are there too. The subject lines range from *Missed you!* to *COME FOR SUPPER??* Henry will be back from vacation in less than ten days. "I've got things under control," I told him before he left. "I can manage without your advice."

"Prove it," he said.

I don't have to prove anything to him but I'll be forced to listen to his "I told you so" if he returns after summer vacation and I've done nothing about Francis and the People for Privacy. The last time I went to see the Chief Librarian about Francis, it backfired on me. This time it's different. He has to listen to me now. I've been here almost a year and I still haven't had any access to anything from Special Collections. I open my office door to head to an appointment with the Chief and almost bump into Edith.

"Why didn't you answer when I knocked earlier?" she says.

"I must have been on the phone. How was your holiday?"

We're boxed into a corner between my office door and the stairwell. Edith moves closer and squeezes me up against my door. "My holidays would have been better if you came with me like you promised. I'll take a hug instead of an excuse." She wraps her arms around me, buries her face in my shirt then gazes up at me. "What did you do all summer?" she asks.

I move her away from me. "I read and wrote reports."

"Am I in your report?" she says.

I turn the knob of the stairwell door. "I have to go now."

She pushes on the door. "I'll walk with you." She follows me down the three flights, each twenty steps, plus the four landings. "I suppose you were writing reports on the weekends too, were you?"

I hold the door open for her at the bottom of the stairwell. "I was busy, yes."

"Why don't we go for lunch together?" she says.

I look at my watch as we stand together outside the Chief Librarian's office. "I have a meeting now. We'll be in touch." I wave goodbye then open the door. His secretary Margaret is on the telephone. She puts the caller on hold. "I'll let you know when he's ready." She continues her phone conversation. "You have to knead it until every breath of air is out of it," she says. "Put it in a warm place near the stove, wrap it in blankets and let it rise again." Silence. "There'll be a crust on the top. It'll have air bubbles inside like a sponge." Silence. "You won't have much left over. Fry it up with a bit of lard, put some molasses on it then have it with your tea." Silence. She gazes at me with the receiver to her ear. "Just a second."

I stand up for emphasis. "Any idea when he'll be finished?"

"Won't be long now," she says then goes back to her call. "I forgot to say, check the best-before date on the Fleischman's yeast before you buy it."

The Chief's door finally opens. He walks out with his arm around Francis. They're talking about tee-off times. Francis hurries by without even looking at me.

"Come in, Carl," the Chief says.

He sits behind his desk. I sit opposite. The office door is still open behind me. He rearranges papers while he speaks to me and to Margaret. "Something came up. I can't talk for long – meeting of deans and directors. Margaret?" he calls out. "Get John on the phone. Tell him to meet me in the lobby before the meeting." He turns to face me. "We need to talk about this project of yours. The Biblio Project, is it? Catchy name." The phone rings. "Hello. John? Car's in with a brake problem again. Can I get a lift with you?" He looks at me while he listens to John. "Give me ten minutes. Fine. Five minutes. Right. Bye."

He moves the phone out of the way, scratches his neck, then his ear. "Sorry about that. Margaret said you want to discuss your project. I have a meeting in a couple of weeks with the People for Privacy. Margaret? When's the privacy group meeting? Twenty-second?"

An Imperfect Librarian

She pokes her head in his office door to confirm.

"I spoke with Francis just now. They're nearly finished the policy draft. They're a hard-working and committed group. I'll certainly give them credit for that. Where is my copy of that privacy policy?" He goes to the filing cabinet, opens drawers, then returns to his desk. "Come to think of it, I don't have time to look at it now. John's on his way. Be thankful you don't have problems with your rotors. Sometimes they'll sand them down for you. That's a lot cheaper. Cost me nearly a thousand dollars for the last visit. They should have insurance for car–"

"I wanted to run some ideas by you about my project."

He lays his briefcase on his desk. When he opens it, he blocks my view of his face. All I can see are his hands shuffling papers in and out of the case.

"Forget about the project. We need to talk about other things now. Once that policy is adopted, we'll have to follow through on the recommendations. Digital Systems will have an important role to play there. You'll enjoy working with Francis. He's a sharp tack for sure. We didn't promote him to Head of Special Collections for nothing. He's been nominated by some librarian's council somewhere, did you know that?"

"What do you mean about working with Francis?"

He stands while he stuffs papers into his case. "What did I do with that folder? There it is." He throws something inside then eyes me over the top of his glasses. "Why don't you see Margaret to set up a time for a long chat?" He fights with his briefcase to make it close.

I stand and rest my hands on his desk. "There are serious problems with how Special Collections operates. I heard what happened with William Myrick. There's a connection with Francis there. I can find the connection if you give me some time."

He leaves his chair then takes his jacket from the coat rack. "I'm out of town for a few weeks."

I follow him out into Margaret's office.

"Make an appointment for Dr. Brunet," he says to her. "Nice seeing you, Carl. You look tired. Are you eating right? Margaret, why don't you give him some of the banana bread you brought in yesterday? Holy! Look at the time. John will be ballistic."

Margaret stands behind her desk with the receiver in one hand. With the other, she offers me a piece of stale banana bread like an edible apology.

CHAPTER THIRTY

caution: potholes ahead

W HEN THE COOK CALLS IN early September, I don't
remember who he is. "Your pal Kelly put you onto
me," he says. We agree to meet at the coffee shop in
a bookstore near campus. When I arrive, he's already there
with a mini smorgasbord of cakes and pies regaled before
him. Behind me, there's a woman on a loveseat reading a book
to a toddler. "I think I can, I think I can," she says to the child.
A group of women laugh and talk in the corner. They're
wearing t-shirts that say *The Book Bags*. At another table, two
people hold newspapers in front of their faces.

"How are ya?" he says. He has a moustache of whipped
cream. "I got some real nice stuff for you."

I sit opposite him. "I hope you're not referring to
the cake."

He points the fork towards me. "Wanna taste?"

I shake my head. "How about if we get right to business?"

"You calls the shots. You gotta pay for the bill here today
though. That's part of my expenses. I runs a tight business.

Money first, pictures after. A hundred bucks."

I sift through the twenty-dollar bills in my wallet. "I think I have that here."

He leans forward over the remains of his feast of pies and cakes, glances side to side then whispers. "You carry five hundred bucks with you all the time?"

I close my wallet. "One hundred dollars per photo? You told me when I hired you, pay on delivery of the goods, but, to be honest, I forgot about you. I haven't heard from you in months. I don't know if I want the photos anymore. Things were different then–"

"If you don't want to see no pictures of her with him, fine with me." He lays a small white envelope on the table near some spilled cream.

"I'll be back in fifteen or twenty minutes," I tell him. On my drive to the nearest bank machine, I pass a stampeding herd of joggers, a man pushing a shopping cart over-filled with recycling, and a *Caution: potholes ahead* sign. I arrive at the shopping mall, drive round and round until I find a place to park then head inside. I stand fourth in line, thinking I should make Henry pay half given that it was his idea to hire the cook in the first place. I wait third in line, trying not to imagine what could be in the photos. When I'm second in line, I think maybe I should stop before I do something I'll regret later.

"It's your turn," the man behind me says.

When I reach the lights at the intersection, I have a choice between a left to the office or a right to the coffee shop where the cook is waiting for me. The light changes colour. A horn blares. The cook is onto pie with ice cream by the time I'm back at his table. The envelopes change hands. He sifts through the contents. I lay my envelope on my lap to open it discreetly. Five hundred dollars for five photos, each taken on the one day, in the parking lot, in his car. One shot of him getting in, one of her, one inside of silhouettes, one of each getting out of the car. I put them back into the envelope. "Is that it? Five hundred dollars? Is that all you can give me?"

He wipes his finger across the plate then licks the ice cream off it. "Yup. That's a good deal! By the way, I can't work for you no more. I'm on another job." He stands to leave. "Don't bother with the cake. Too dry. Pie's too watery. Good luck to you. See ya later." The waitress returns. He reaches into his pocket, pulls out a ten-dollar bill, lays it in her hand. "A little tip for you." He's gone before she has a chance to thank him. The waitress gives me his bill.

"Are you sure it costs this much?" I ask.

She studies the slip of paper then goes behind the counter. I get up from the table, stroll over to the till and read the posters taped on the wall while I wait.

RALLY FOR READERS' RIGHTS
Saturday, September 28th, 2000
Churchill Square Soccer Field
www.protectprivacy.blogger.com

The waitress returns. "You're right," she says. "He had two pies, not one. It's actually $5.59 more."

On my way out the door, I pass a recycling bin then a trash can. I throw the receipt for his food in one and the photos in the other. I pull my collar up around my neck for protection against the sheets of rain blowing sideways across the parking lot. I sit behind the wheel and watch drops splatter onto the windshield. Mercedes and Cyril swear by the *Farmer's Almanac*, which predicts a harsh winter ahead. "Summer's over now," Cyril said. "Time to pay for it."

CHAPTER THIRTY-ONE

the crimson hexagon

I T'S ONE OF THOSE CLOUDY nights when the star-lights don't live up to their name. Norah's been sleeping for hours. I'll never catch up with her. This is not the first time I've gone downstairs when I should normally be asleep. The nightlight on the stairs is kind on the eyes. In the kitchen, there's more shadow than light. I add a log to the stove then turn the fan on high to take the chill out of the damp fall air. The dogs stir in the porch. Three noses and six eyes appear in the glass. I ignore their scratching and whining. They settle once they realize I won't open any doors for them.

I browse her bookshelves for something to make me sleepy. There's Arthur Rackham's illustrations of *Grimm's Fairy Tales*, *Peter Pan*, *The Wind in the Willows* and *A Midsummer Night's Dream*. I've seen them before but they're more haunting without the bright light of day. It's an expensive volume with glossy pages and an embossed cover. I flip to the front for information about the edition. That's when I notice the bookplate.

The dogs bark suddenly. I jump. I slide the book into its place on the shelf then go to the porch. A piece of wood falls off the woodpile. Quarto bolts to the side then tips over a bowl of water that spills on the floor. I pull them away from the door so I can open it. Hardened leaves cut against my bare feet. Just as I'm closing the door, the door of the Crimson Hexagon opens. A silhouette appears then disappears.

I throw on my boots and jacket. Outside, the moon slides from behind a patch of cloud. I follow the path. The dogs sniff at the entrance. I press down on the handle but it's locked. No one answers when I knock. I blow into my hands then bury them in my pocket. Before I head back to her house, I check the barn. His Jaguar is parked next to my lemon. The trees make a whooshing sound. The waves respond with a crash. I remember the images from Rackham's book: trees with outstretched arms, tiny men with long thin hands larger than their heads, translucent skin over bones without flesh, "spotted snakes with double tongue," and drowned bodies floating into the outstretched arms of water nymphs.

The dogs think I'm playing with them when they see me running to the house. The four of us crowd into the porch. They shake as if they're getting rid of water on their coats. I open the porch door then close it quickly behind me to keep the heat in. Octavo yelps. I go down on my hands and knees. "Sorry, Octavo. Poor dog. I didn't mean to trap your paw." The other two poke their wets noses in my face. A tongue licks my ear. Octavo wags his tail. I give him a final pat then close the door carefully. The nightlight guides my way up the stairs to the peak until I'm under the covers next to her warm body. "Francis is here," I whisper. She doesn't stir.

It's quiet in the peak by her side. I fall asleep thinking about Rackham's goblins, gremlins and trees with eyes and ears. They don't haunt my dreams. The dogs do. They're barking, herding me into the waves. Norah appears in the window in the peak. She puts her tongue in Francis' mouth. An explosion frightens the dogs away. I turn to face a giant wave with the face of a monster. Pots clang in the kitchen, dogs bark and I'm saved. It's morning. Outside, the sky and water are a colour of blue that denies there'd ever been darkness. No wind is blowing, no waves are crashing but the dogs are still barking.

I sit at the kitchen table and put on my socks. "Aren't you going to do something about them? They were barking in my dream. They're always barking."

She unloads a fistful of utensils from the dishwasher. "Good morning to you too."

"Sorry. I'd call the dogs myself but they don't listen to me."

She hands me a glass of juice then goes back to her kitchen chores. "Did they listen to you when they were barking in your dream?"

I'd nearly forgotten about that dream. "I saw Francis go into the Crimson Hexagon in the middle of the night."

She doesn't say anything. She goes to the bathroom. I get my breakfast. The toilet flushes then the door opens. She takes a broom from the closet and sweeps the floor.

"Don't you think it's a bit odd to have him around here at two or three in the morning?"

She doesn't look at me while she sweeps. "I don't bother to think about it."

An Imperfect Librarian

I cut some bread and put it in the toaster. "Why do you have to be evasive about it?"

She goes to the closet for the dustpan. "You see it as evasive," she says. "I see it as answering your question the best I can."

I move out of her way and sit at the table again. "Why don't you come out and say what your relationship is with him?"

This time she stops what she's doing and looks directly at me. "Not so early in the day, please."

How can the day be early if the night was so long? Every time I woke, it seemed like another night. "You could be more–"

"I don't expect you to be more of anything." The toast pops. She puts it on a plate and lays it in front of me.

"Why can't you trust me, Norah? How can we be together if you're hiding things?"

She goes to the porch. "Why can't you trust me? How can we be together if you have to satisfy every ounce of curiosity–"

"Are you saying you don't want to be together?"

She pulls her jacket on over her sweater. "I'm saying I enjoyed our summer together but for now I have more important things to do than satisfy your idle curiosity. My application for tenure is due next week, I'm teaching three large classes. I'm already under enough stress without you pressuring me."

I stand up from the table to face her. "Idle curiosity? Is that how you see it?"

She's rummaging in the porch looking for something. "Either that or you need to go away and deal with your problem."

"I've heard that one before."

"Maybe it's time you listened to their advice," she says.

"Not when it comes from someone I don't trust."

She opens the door partway. "Trust has a self-fulfilling character about it."

"Exactly."

"I have to feed the horses, bring the dogs to the vet for shots, et cetera, et cetera. I have my hands full with more than I can cope with, and, to be honest, since I know that's something you demand of me, I don't have time for a relationship where trust is an issue."

She pulls the door sharply to a close, like an exclamation mark jabbed onto the page with the fine point of a pencil.

CHAPTER THIRTY-TWO

quotation marks

I'D BEEN WISHING FOR A hostile Saturday with raging winds, rain on the verge of a breakdown, the kind of day when people are warned to go out only for emergencies. Instead, the temperature and the colour of the sky are record-breaking. It's ideal weather for rowing on the pond or visiting a cove. Everyone is looking for an excuse to be outdoors and what better excuse than the People for Privacy rally? I arrive just as it's ending.

Francis works the crowd with the charm and conviction of a politician. "Personal freedoms have to be safeguarded!" he shouts.

I wear a baseball hat, sunglasses and Cyril's old fly-fishing vest over a t-shirt to blend into the crowd. I sit on a bench near the side of the field so my height doesn't give me away.

"Monitoring of cellphone use, financial surveillance, insurance companies checking on health information: Our rights and freedoms are threatened every day."

The Frisbee and ball traffic frighten away the birds. The

squeaking sounds of swings and the shouts of children playing interfere like static with his speech.

"The next time someone is entering your information into the computer, ask questions: Who sees your personal information? Is it cross-linked or connected electronically with other information? How will it be used? What are you going to do about it? Protect your information!" He points a finger at the crowd of no more than twenty-five or thirty.

They applaud and chant as they walk away. "Pri-va-cy! Pri-va-cy! Pri-va-cy!"

Someone reaches from behind and cups hands over my sunglasses. "Aren't you a sight with that get-up," Edith says. "Halloween's not for another month." She makes herself comfortable on the bench next to me.

"What did you think of the rally?"

"I think it's a good idea you're disguised," she says. "You should wear those glasses more often. Although, I love your brown eyes." She takes the baseball hat that Cyril lent me and puts it on her head. A gust of wind blows it onto the field. She chases after it. She's out of breath when she hands it back to me.

"What about our friend Francis?" I ask.

"Francis has two friends in the world and I'm not one of them," she says.

"I'm surprised he has that many."

This time, she borrows my glasses. "The Chief is one and the other is you-know-who."

"No idea."

She turns her head side to side checking the view through the glasses. "Norah Myrick is his..." She pauses then imitates quotation marks with her fingers. "Friend." She waves to someone. "Be right back." She hands me my glasses then runs over to a woman. They hug and talk.

An Imperfect Librarian

I stretch my arms over the back of the bench and cross my legs while I wait. Halfway across the field, Francis is stuffing his loudspeaker into a bag. He throws it over his shoulder and walks away with a woman on either side. My arms start to feel stiff so I stand up from the bench. I walk towards the hotdog stand. One of the members of the privacy group goes by. I turn the other way then go back to the bench. The woman Edith is talking to walks away.

"Sorry about that," Edith says to me. She takes her sweater off the park bench and lays it over her shoulder before she sits. "It's cooling down, isn't it?"

"What did you mean by *friend*?"

"Right after her father died, she threatened to sue the library if we didn't give her the original of every shred of paper her father donated to the archives. She said he never meant to leave us the originals and that we, or more so I, took advantage of the fact that he wasn't well. He *was* forgetful. There's no doubt about that. But I'm sure he was in his right mind when he donated the materials."

"How do you make the leap from there to Francis?"

"Put two and two together. As soon as they announced the archives would be merged with Special Collections, we never heard another word from Norah Myrick. Francis more or less took over my position. They claimed I didn't have the resources to manage the archives properly. They didn't know what they were talking about." She waves to someone again. "Just a second." She walks over to talk to a man.

I recognize him from the library and wave. He doesn't recognize me. I lean back on the bench and watch a boys' soccer team. They look like five-year-olds wearing eight-year-olds' uniforms. A man blows a whistle and the boys crowd around him. The parents sit on blankets or fold-up lawn chairs along the sidelines. When I was in school, I wanted to be on a sports team but I didn't bother to try out. "You'll only get hurt," Papa said. He knew from experience what it was like to be too tall, too skinny and too uncoordinated on the field.

"That was Peter Harrison from circulation," Edith says. She reaches her arms into the sleeves of her sweater. "Wife's in chemo. Breast cancer. God help us. Another one."

"Is that it then about Francis' second friend?"

She puts her hands on her waist and turns to face me. "You're some curious, aren't you? What have you been doing all summer? Tell me."

A ball rolls under the bench. I throw it out into the field. "Nothing. Why?"

"Did you visit Blackhead by chance?"

"Maybe."

"It's an itsy-bitsy world. Can't keep secrets from Edie." She nudges me with her shoulder.

"I'm not sure what secrets people in Blackhead have about me."

"You'd be surprised."

"What are you getting at, Edith?"

A young girl passes by with a metal detector. Edith throws a toonie in her path. "Thanks, miss," the girl says.

"You still haven't answered my question about Blackhead, have you?"

"I bought something at the store, yes."

"That's a long way to the corner store when you live on Gower Street."

The girl with the metal detector goes past again. She points it towards Edith. I throw her what I have in my pocket – a dime and a nickel. She ignores them.

"Let's get a hotdog before the guy leaves," Edith says. She grabs my arm to drag me up from the bench. We walk over to the stand and wait in line. We take the two-for-one special, all-dressed. I eat leaning against a tree trunk. A leaf blows into my relish. Someone in the apartment building across the street closes a window. Edith pulls a tissue from her sleeve then wipes the corner of my mouth. "You had a gob of mustard there." The wind rustles the leaves in the branches above our heads. A young couple rolls up their blanket. They lay their toddler in a stroller and jog across the field. I poke my hands in my pockets to warm them. Edith twines her arm into mine. "Come for supper. We'll go downtown afterwards, make a night of it. Just as friends. What do you say?"

"I'm really not in the mood. Thanks, Edith."

She lets go of my arm, looks for something inside her purse, then pulls out her car keys. "Too bad. We would have had a great evening. By the way, you're not the only gentleman who visits my cousin's store in Blackhead for baking powder and ladies' scented soaps."

"What's that supposed to mean?"

She looks over her shoulder as she walks towards the cars lining the road. "That's up to you to decide."

CHAPTER THIRTY-THREE

mis-information services

L ONG BEFORE THE END OF October, scarecrows, pumpkins and skeletons sprout like dandelions in front gardens. Cyril tells me about his plans to install speakers in the front windows to play Halloween sound effects. Mercedes puts a stop to it and they settle on miniature pumpkin lights around the front door. "None for me, thanks anyway, Cyril. No, not around the ceiling pipes either."

At the library, there are no pumpkin lights, though mid-term exams have given students a ghoulish pallor. Reading Room activity is at its peak. I'd expect Henry to be drooling over the view. Instead, he's staring into space, or more rightly, into his coffee cup. I wouldn't be in a good mood either if I'd spent the summer caring for a dying father, if my son and daughter-in-law had split up and my teenage grandson was caught shoplifting cigarettes. "That's the good part," Henry says about his two-month visit to Ireland.

"I bought some new coffee from Auntie Crae's, if that will make you feel any better."

"Since when did you ever brew a cup of coffee that would make anyone feel better?" he says. "You're a fine one to be talking about feeling better. Look at you. You'd think after the beautiful summer here on the island you'd have a ray of sunshine in you but you're dark as the arse of a black hole," he says. "I hope you aren't hanging out with that Reading Room woman, because if you are, I won't help you anymore."

"I'm not seeing Norah Myrick. Elsa's the problem right now. She's split up with her Brutus. She's been sending me emails almost daily."

"Is this the Viking Vixen who cuckolded you with another Amazon? What would she be wanting with the likes of you? Your semen? Don't be letting your sperm go to your head. There's a good one for you."

"I don't know what she wants but I've decided to go to Norway to tie up some loose ends. I'm leaving on the November eleventh long weekend. I'll visit with Tatie and Papa while I'm over there."

"If you asked me, I'd say you're scrounging for an excuse to avoid your priorities."

"Remind me not to ask."

"Sharpening your tongue over the last few months, were you?"

Of all the months, weeks and days, my memory is trapped in the five or ten minutes in Norah's kitchen. *I don't have time for a relationship where trust is an issue*, she said.

"I've been focusing on my priorities more than you realise. I figured out that Francis owns the Crimson Hexagon and that he visits there at odd hours of the morning, that—"

"You're the one who knows most about how our information is managed. Once that privacy policy is passed, you could find yourself with a new title: Dr. Carl Brunet, Data and Information Control Manager, Privacy Protection Services for the King Edward University Library, Lackey for Francis Hickey. Will you like that, with Francis for your boss? 'Yes, Mr. Hickey. Sorry, Mr. Hickey. Right away, Mr. Hickey. Lick your ass, Mr. Hickey?'"

"More like, 'Stay off my case, Mr. Hickey. Hand over the Special Collections inventory, Mr. Hickey.'"

"I applied for the position of Head of Special Collections when it came up three years ago. I should have been the obvious choice. I'd been here longer. I have more experience," Henry says.

"Why did they give it to him?"

"Because he sucks as much as he fucks. I challenged him once. He was presenting a report on Special Collections to Library Council. He put forward a motion to approve a fifteen percent increase in his budget. I argued against it but Francis knew how to manipulate them. He cracked a lame joke that had everyone laughing at my expense. Something about the likes of Irishmen working at 'Mis-information Services.'"

"A fifteen percent increase to do fifteen percent more of what?"

"Everyone assumes the Reading Room's a bastion, an Alcatraz, with its fancy security features, the no touching this, no copying that. The real threat is the Trojan horse on the inside. He struts around the library, Head of the People for Privacy, protecting the public good, defender of basic rights. My fucking belly he is." Henry grabs his belly, one hand on either side and shakes it. "It's about time someone pruned the prick."

I turn away from the view of the Reading Room to face him. "Let me get this straight, Henry. Are you trying to rehabilitate me and save my project or are you simply–"

"All that boring Bibliomining banter. I have more sympathy for this privacy stuff. As for rehabilitating you, the curve is steep," he says, his arm raised up before him as if I couldn't understand without the gesture.

An Imperfect Librarian

CHAPTER THIRTY-FOUR

through the looking glass

FTER MEGABYTES OF *MESSAGE BLOCKED for this recipient,* followed by my declined invitation to share fatherhood with Brutus, Elsa announces that she misses her husband, me, Carl Brunet, recent recipient of the outstanding-cuckolded-husband-of-all-time award. The same Carl Brunet who'll soon have a hint of a lean to one side from poking his hand in his pocket to rub the two smooth beach rocks between his fingers.

I squander a fortune on an overpriced ticket, dump what clean clothes I own into a backpack then board the plane for a weekend in Norway. I forget to ask for an aisle seat to avoid the aerial view of the ponds and meadows that remind me so much of Cliffhead. When I arrive in Heathrow, I visit a bookstore while I wait for my connection to Oslo. I end up in the history section even though I never read history books. I walk past the duty-free shop with its promotion on cognac. I'm tempted to ask if they know how well it mixes with partridgeberries. I fall asleep on the plane until the bumpy landing in Oslo jolts me awake. The passengers push to debark. I stay behind, half-asleep, half-wondering how I ended up on the other half of the world.

In the terminal, I waste time walking to the baggage claim. Elsa's at the end of the corridor. It's not easy to ignore someone so tall, so blond and so pressed up against the glass wall. She waves. I look the other way. I didn't check in any baggage but I stand around the carousel anyway. One by one, the bags disappear until I'm facing an empty carousel.

"Did you get your luggage?" a man in a uniform asks.

As soon as I exit the baggage area, she flaps her arms around me. "It's good to see you," she says. "You're still wearing that same shirt and pants. Have you been losing weight?"

"I've shed a bit. Life's hard in Newfoundland. I have to fight to stay alive."

She glares at me. "Is this a joke you're doing?"

I almost forgot that Elsa hasn't mastered the nuances of English. "Yes. I'm making a joke."

"You weren't a joker before. You always…" She talks about how I used to be, how she used to be and how we're going to be. We ride the elevator to the parking lot. Elsa updates me on the last two years. "…then there was this one time when Sophie wanted me to…" I'm distracted by our reflections in the mirrored sides of the elevator – infinite layers of Carl and Elsa reflecting off each other. She curls her fingers into mine as the elevator descends. I pull away to adjust the bag on my shoulder. The door opens. I follow her through a maze of parked cars.

"Why don't I stay with you at your hotel?" she says. "I'm your wife. I hope you have not forgot this already."

I shake my head. "*Forgot* is not the word."

She chats about who we'll visit, invitations to suppers, how happy she is to see me, how we're going to enjoy the old times together. I interrupt the old times to ask her about new times. "Do you know if I'll have email access in my hotel room?"

She laughs. "You don't need email while you're here. You'll be too busy. Tonight, we'll have something to eat, talk about old times, I'll help you unpack, give you a massage."

She unlocks her car and I take my seat in the front. "I'm not hungry and I don't need to unpack but I do need to send an email."

"Once you smell the food, you'll rediscover your appetite – same for your wife."

"I don't want to be married to you anymore, Elsa. I decided on the way over here that I want a divorce."

"What are you talking about all of a sudden? You can't decide something so important on an airplane flight!"

I gaze out through the side window. "Sorry. I had time to think about what I want. It's not you. It's not a life in Norway."

Her sniffles harmonize with the swishing sound of the wipers. "Are you planning to stay forever in Newfieland?" she says.

"I promise to stop calling her Brutus if you'll stop calling Newfoundland, Newfieland."

Elsa drives the car and the argument for the full distance to the hotel. When we arrive, she parks then unfastens her seatbelt. "You are always saying you will do anything for me to be happy. I want to be with my husband. Please."

The two palm-sized beach rocks are in my pocket. I rub them between my fingers. "Goodnight, Elsa. See you tomorrow. Call before you come."

The bellboy opens the hotel door and greets me.

I ask him if they have Internet access. The connection turns out to be slow but my message goes through anyway.

Norah,

…just arrived in Oslo to take care of some personal affairs…will be in Newfoundland late Monday afternoon…I wanted to tell you…I'm sorry for not trusting you…I miss you…I love you…

C…

CHAPTER THIRTY-FIVE

mor, far, datter & sønn

THE TELEPHONE WAKES ME. IT'S not the woman in my dream. While Elsa talks, I check my email: eleven marketing penis-lengthening apparatus, fourteen offering an advanced degree without study, fifteen messages from Nigerian scam artists, twenty-one offers of cheap prescription drugs and one message from Norah.

> *Hello Carl,*
> *You missed a spectacular fall at Cliffhead. Folio*
> *injured herself. She was asking for you ;>) The tail of*
> *Hurricane Juan ripped shingles off my roof. No damage*
> *to books :>) I missed you too :>(If the snow holds off,*
> *we can fit in a few beach bonfires. Lots to look forward*
> *to :>I (That's meant to represent a big smile).*
> *Norah*
> *p. s. Tolerance of ambiguity helps in a relationship.*

Elsa calls me from her car in the hotel parking lot. "I'm on my way to your room."

I jump out of bed and put on my trousers. "No point. I'm just going out the door now."

We meet in the squatty lobby of the hotel. She tells me the plan for the next forty-eight hours. I tell her that I want to see a lawyer about the divorce. She's standing next to a couple from Germany, in front of the desk staff and not far from the man she left for another woman. She shouts: "You ask me, 'Come back to you!' For two years, 'Come back to me, Elsa. Come back.' Now you're tired and you wake complaining, 'I want a divorce. I want a divorce.'"

Everyone is staring at us. I turn to face the door. "Is your car out front, Elsa? We can talk there."

She's frozen in the middle of the lobby, playing the space like centre stage. She raises her hands to her face. "Talk about what? A divorce?"

The bellboy opens the door for me. "We'll discuss it in the car, OK?"

It's cold outside, even colder than in my basement flat during those sombre nights when I slept without the body of my wife beside me. Finally, she comes out of the hotel and unlocks the car. "Many couples separate for a period, resume the marriage later and it's much better," she says while she plays with the car keys in her lap.

"We're not one of those *many* couples."

"When I met Sophie, I thought she was what I needed."

I take the keys from her lap to put them in the ignition. The sooner we start moving, the sooner I'll see a lawyer, the sooner I see a lawyer, the closer I'll be to–

"Then I realized I did not want to be with Sophie or with any woman. I wanted to be with my husband and…"

I turn to face her. "What?"

She looks out the windshield. "If we don't have our children now it will be too late. I became forty this year. You're fifty. How much longer can you wait? You don't want to be seventy with a ten-year-old. We'll make an excellent child together. Your dark colour. My fair colour. Our child will be unique. You're well-educated. I'm a skilled athlete."

"A well-educated, dark father? Is that what I represent for you? I don't want children. I don't want to be married to you. I can't believe I was so naïve."

It's Saturday morning, not yet eleven o'clock and I have a headache. In Cliffhead, it's even earlier but I bet the dogs have been up for a couple of hours. Norah is probably sitting at the kitchen table reading the newspaper and drinking coffee under the orange glow of the lamp. The horses have already been fed but the barn will need to be shovelled out. She might take a ride on Biblio as far as the pond to check on Ray's traps. Maybe she'll do some work on the rock wall bordering the path. If it's raining, she might sit and read in front of the windows in the living room with the woodstove on high and the dogs settled in the porch.

Elsa plays with the keys. The car feels stuffy. The windows are fogging up from the inside. It's grey outside. "We can seek help from a marriage counsellor," she says.

I take the keys from her lap and put them in the ignition "Not unless he specializes in speedy divorces. Let's go."

For the rest of the day, I dodge references to "our children." Elsa's friends greet us with "so happy to see you two together again." Her parents tell me "glad you decided to come back," in the spirit of *we forgive you*. That night, I call Norah. She tells me about how Folio broke her leg when she came too close to Walter's horse. I ask her what she's been doing for the last five weeks. She talks about what a great year it's been for berries. "Wait till you see all the jars of jam," she says. She had her roof re-shingled but now there's a leak in the living room. We talk about what we'll do under the star-lights besides gazing at the sky.

Day two, Sunday: I spend the morning on the phone trying to contact a lawyer. We stop by the university but the corridors are empty. We stroll downtown. Mercedes asked for a souvenir spoon of Oslo and I want to buy a book for Norah. The streets are almost empty except for tourists. The wind is cold. Elsa twines her arm in mine. She tries to detour me to stores where they sell baby items. We walk down the road where her office is located. I remember how often I paced the sidewalks hoping to run into her. Now, I'm trying to find an excuse to not be with her. I propose the most unromantic meal I can think of.

Elsa would normally never eat in a fast food outlet, but she makes an exception this time. We sit in a booth with red plastic seats under fluorescent lights, eating French fries with ketchup, coleslaw and greasy deep-fried chicken. I'd prefer a fish, chips, dressing and gravy from the Campus Quaff any day. I tell her about St. John's and how everyone knows everyone. I describe the time I saw a moose and her calf on the road to Cape Spear and about the time when I was wading in the ocean and the capelin washed in over my feet. I explain about the winds and how quickly the temperature can change.

Elsa rolls her eyes and pushes her half-eaten supper away from her. "You complain that I talk too much about babies. What do I care about weather in Newfoundland?"

I lie in bed that night in the dark after an argument with Elsa and a conversation with Norah. I can almost pretend I'm back on Gower Street. Maybe the flat is not so bad after all. If I moved out I wouldn't see Cyril and Mercedes as much. Although, I wouldn't mind if it meant living at Cliffhead. I'd invite them to visit. The four of us would sit around in the evening and play trivia or cards. Mercedes would be impressed with Norah's kitchen and Cyril would love the dogs. Years before I met them, they used to own a Labrador retriever. It darted into the road after a pigeon and was killed by a car. Cyril has a cabin rented in a national park for a weekend in May. Maybe Norah can come with us. She told me she likes fishing. I fall asleep dreaming about a rowboat floating on a pond with the trout jumping out of the water after flies, the white-throated sparrows calling to each other and two people lying in the bottom of the rowboat in each other's arms.

The following morning, Elsa drives me fifty kilometres to catch my plane. The theme of her conversation hasn't changed. "I don't mind giving you some time to think about it," she says. "I can visit you this spring."

As far as I can tell, there is no such thing as spring in Newfoundland beyond the lull at the end of winter when all the snow is nearly melted except for piles in the parking lots. There are those rare days when it's so warm you can lie in a rowboat, dangle your feet over the edge or sit at the top of a cliff and admire the icebergs.

When we arrive at the airport, we take the same route we followed three days earlier, though in reverse: through the maze of parked cars, up the elevator with our reflections in the mirrored walls all the way to the security gate.

"Goodbye. Good luck with Sophie. Tell your parents thanks for the fine meal at their home on Saturday night. Thanks to Marlene for the luncheon."

She tugs on my shirt. "Your flight is not for another forty-five minutes. Stay with me here. We can talk."

I throw my backpack over my shoulder, pick up my laptop then walk towards the queue of passengers. "Not unless the conversation is about completing the paperwork for the divorce. You're only prolonging matters, making them more complicated and costly."

Elsa follows by my side. "My husband wants to divorce me, does not want to have children. What about that cost?"

"I'll say hello to Papa and Tatie for you."

"How will they feel when they learn that their only child is not planning to give them any grandchildren?"

"Tatie's not my mother. You know that. The lawyer will be in touch."

I stop, then turn to face her before I go through security. "One last question – it's just a little poll I've been doing. If you were in a situation where all the books in the world were going to be destroyed and you wanted to memorize one for future generations what would it be?"

"There won't be future generations if people like you and me don't have children."

"Assuming there were, what book would you choose?"

"You wonder why I'm always talking about babies. I wonder why you're talking about books. What's wrong with you?"

"I'm curious that's all. Name one book you believe should be passed on."

"I've been reading so many lately, I'm not sure which I'd pick. There's Dr. Spock but he's–"

I bend forward quickly and kiss her on the cheek. "Thanks, Elsa. Makes sense. Bye." I step forward into security. The glass door slides shut behind me.

CHAPTER THIRTY-SIX

georges & georgette

F ROM OSLO TO PARIS THEN to the Gare du Nord, I don't waste a step. Papa will be upset if I'm late. I arrive right on time just as the TGV pokes its aristocratic nose into the station. The porter motions us to move aside. Brakes squeak, whistles blow, people swarm around the opening doors. I sort through the passengers: tired backpackers, rushed businessmen, dazed tourists, eager immigrants and weekend commuters. There's no sign of Georges and Georgette – twins in their seventies.

"Is this the train from Avignon?" I ask a backpacker. He nods. Finally, I see them. They're moving slowly with their heads lowered. Tatie is holding onto Papa. I call to them but they turn in the wrong direction. "Papa! Tatie! It's Carl. Over here!" I wave then elbow a path towards them.

Tatie reaches for me with her arms outstretched like someone about to fall. "Don't squeeze me too hard," she says. "Look at you. All the way from Canada."

Papa gives me an official peck on both cheeks. "Five o'clock this morning we left Cavaillon. We spent an hour stuck in traffic then we almost missed the train. Georgette read the schedule wrong. She was looking at the weekend schedule instead of Monday's."

Tatie smacks Papa on the arm. "Stop talking about that. Say hello to him."

We push through the crowds. We pass by the signs for taxis, busses, metro, parking, then by the massive arrivals and departure board that stretches to the ceiling. Tatie lets go of my arm. She rests her fragile fingers on my cheeks then draws my head down to kiss me. I catch a trace of the wintergreen ointment she uses for her arthritis. The knuckles on her fingers are swollen. Her veins are visible through the skin. We go outside the gloomy station to scout for a place to eat and plan our day together.

"After the train arrived, I was afraid I mixed up the times. I couldn't remember if you said you were staying in Avignon yesterday or today." We cross the street in front of the station, watching for taxis, motorcyclists and careless Parisian drivers.

Papa responds before Tatie. "You worry and forget exactly like Georgette. One in my life would be plenty, but I have both of you." The hump in his back is bigger than the last time I saw him. The whites of his eyes are yellowish.

"You didn't forget," Tatie says. "We'll stay the night in Avignon, go to the market tomorrow morning then drive home in the afternoon."

Papa interrupts. "Who decided that we're going to the market tomorrow morning? If she's not spending money in Avignon, she's not happy."

We choose the closest Bistro. A waitress leads us to a table. Papa and Tatie ask for cappuccino with croissants and Swiss cheese on the side. Twins with matching food. When our order arrives, Papa says to the waitress, "If I'd known it was going to take that long, I would have ordered lunch." Tatie doesn't flinch at the comment. The waitress apologizes. Papa cuts open Tatie's croissant for her then folds the cheese inside. Her own hands are too crippled to do it.

"You must come visit," I tell them.

Papa talks to the sandwich in front of his face. "I've done my reading about Newfoundland. No need to hear about or go there."

"You can't know a place by reading about it anymore than you can know a person by reading about them."

"Depends on the quality of the reading material," he says.

"What can you glean from an Internet site or an encyclopaedia?"

He stops eating to stare at me. "Who said anything about encyclopaedias?"

"OK. So, *Fodor's*, Newfoundland. Really, Papa."

"I'm talking about novels, not travel books: *The Shipping News, Random Passage, The Colony of Unrequited Dreams.*"

"Did you read those?"

"I read about them. They summed up the themes," he says.

"That's not the same as being there."

"I've lived in Canada too, don't forget," he says.

"Newfoundland is not the same as Canada."

Tatie swallows a bite, takes a drink of coffee then says, "In the village, they call your Papa *Le Canadien* to make fun of his tales about the wolves and Indians of Canada."

"Not true. They call me *Le Canadien* because most of them have never been farther than Avignon."

"What about me?" Tatie asks. "I've been off the continent. And you're leaving out Monsieur Giroux. He had a military posting in Vietnam. Donnatina, the butcher's wife, was born in Naples. And you're forgetting about Maximillian. He lived in Germany before the war."

"I'm talking about people who've been to Canada," he says.

Papa spent six years there. If I didn't know better I'd say it was more like sixty, and more like living in the woods trading furs with North American natives than on the tenth floor of an apartment building in Quebec City, trying unsuccessfully to write a doctoral dissertation. I don't remember much about those days except that I had to stay in my room. He always made sure I had more than enough to read.

Tatie changes the subject. "What about Elsa? Is it completely over? You're not too old to have children."

"Elsa and I will be divorced once the paperwork is finished. There's nothing more to say except I met someone in Newfoundland who–"

"No son of mine will marry an English woman."

"Stop interrupting him," Tatie says.

"Me interrupting? What are you doing? And I'm not going shopping in Avignon on Sunday."

"Stop, please! I'm friends with a woman. Her name is Norah. She lives by the ocean. We've been hiking and horseback riding. I've been learning how to swim, row on the pond–"

"Be careful you don't catch pneumonia, or worse, drown. You're practically in the Arctic."

"Come on, Tatie. You're exaggerating."

"Georgette doesn't understand about latitude and longitudes," says Papa.

"You're a fine one to talk," Tatie says. "What do you know about geography? You're not an expert."

"And you're not an expert on experts," Papa says.

I'd already made a mental list of anecdotes I planned to share with them. There was the time when I was in a restaurant with Edith and she introduced me to the premier of the province. Apparently, her brother used to play hockey with

An Imperfect Librarian

him. I want to tell them about when Mercedes and Cyril held a surprise birthday party for my fiftieth, complete with party hats, cake, gifts and a card that said *Happy 60th*. I'm sure Cyril was joking. I want to tell them about when Norah and I were riding on the side of the road to Cape Spear and the horses were spooked by a motorcycle. But there's no room in the conversation. After so many years of listening to them contradicting each other like Tweedledee and Tweedledum, I should have predicted there wouldn't be.

CHAPTER THIRTY-SEVEN

not-so-great britain

T HE WAITRESS REMOVES OUR CUPS and plates then sets the table for the next customers. Papa and Tatie lean back in their chairs so they're not in her way but they don't pick up on her cues that it's time for us to leave. We can't leave because we can't agree where to go. Shopping is out of the question. We can't travel by metro because Tatie is worried about pickpockets. She won't allow me to hold onto her bag. It's hidden under her coat in her lap. Museums are not possible because Papa insists he doesn't want to visit any place where there might be crowds of Brits.

"What's so great about them?" he says. "You don't hear us pretending to be Great France or the Germans, Great Germany."

"Where do you want to go?" I ask. "Please tell me."

"If they were satisfied with simply Britain, I could have tolerated them," he says. "I could have tolerated Philip. But no. They're the Great British. They eat fried potatoes wrapped in a newspaper. As a citizen of Great France, I prefer to read my newspapers, not eat out of them."

Tatie's ex-husband, Philip, is to Tatie what the sciatic nerve problem is to Henry. The mere mention of his name makes her wince. She married him to spite Papa. That's my theory. He was from not-so-great Britain and they turned out to be a not-so-great match. She refused to speak English with Philip in the same way she refused to speak English with me. When he'd come home late, Tatie would complain. One day, he didn't come home at all. For two weeks after that, Tatie slept on the couch in the front room waiting for him. I'd wake to go to the bathroom, hear her crying and think it had something to do with me. I'd sit with her and hold her hand to make up for the times I'd told her, "You're not my mother!"

"If you can't agree on a place to go, we'll have to stay here," I tell them. "That means we'll need to order something."

Tatie shakes her head. "I'm not the one who's disagreeing. It's your Papa."

"That's because you want to go shopping," he says.

"Not in Paris, I don't want to go shopping," Tatie says. "There are too many pickpockets. Besides, we're going shopping at the market tomorrow."

"You do want to go shopping. You don't want to go shopping. Make up your mind."

I call the waitress to the table and order more coffee. She turns to Papa. "And for your wife, Monsieur?"

Papa: If she was my wife, I would have divorced her long ago.

Tatie: I never would have married you in the first place so you couldn't have divorced me.

The waitress is unfazed by the conversation. She leaves. They continue to ricochet off each other.

Tatie: We're growing old, Carl.

Papa: I'm not as old as you.

Tatie: Ten minutes makes little difference in a lifetime.

Papa: It made a difference to me. With you born and me

NOT-SO-GREAT BRITAIN

still in the womb, I had the place to myself.

Tatie: The pleasure was all mine.

I change the conversation to the only topic they'll agree on: the state of the country. Papa complains about how, if France adopts a common European currency, it will be the end of the nation. Tatie says they won't be able to afford to keep the house. Papa launches into a tirade about how voters should have elected Le Penn. Tatie says they might have to get rid of the car if gas prices go up. I leave them together to map out the future of life in France while I pay the bill.

We leave the Bistro then visit the information counter in the station. The attendant suggests an afternoon tour on a double-decker bus with hop-on-and-off visits throughout Paris. Tatie is fine with the idea but Papa insists it's out of the question. He doesn't want to drive around Paris with a bunch of Great Brits. I reassure him. "I'll find us seats in an area of the bus without them."

We leave the train station, buy the tickets and board the bus. There's a tour group on the bottom floor where it's comfortable and warm. They're wearing baseball hats with *Liverpool Seniors' Club*. We go to the upper deck. Papa and Tatie sit together. I take the seat behind them. Before the bus leaves, I pull the gifts out of my backpack: a Newfoundland hand-knit woollen scarf for Tatie, gloves for Papa. He wraps the scarf around Tatie's neck then puts the gloves on her hands before he reaches his arm around her.

We put on our headsets. The three-hour circuit tour begins: Le Louvre, l'Hôtel de Ville, La Bastille, La Sorbonne, St. Germain-des-Prés, Les Champs-Elysées, l'Arc de Triomphe, La Tour Eiffel, Invalides. It's too much trouble for Papa and Tatie to climb up and down the stairs so we stay on the bus when it makes its stops. I take advantage of the opportunity to conduct my *Fahrenheit 451* poll. I move into the seat in front of them

An Imperfect Librarian

then turn partway around to face them. "You have to imagine a scenario where there'll be no more books and you have an opportunity to memorize one to share with future generations."

Papa shakes his head. "I don't have to imagine anything."

"What about you, Tatie? What would your book be?"

"I'm too old to be memorizing."

"Come on! Think of something," I plead.

"*Fables and Tales of the Middle Ages*," she replies.

"That's exactly what I'd memorize."

"What's the point if two people choose the same book?" Papa asks.

"It's hypothetical, Papa. The point is simply to see what people believe needs to be passed on."

"If that's the case, I pick *France: The Greatest Nation*."

"Is that a book?" I ask.

"It's a book and it's the truth."

"I thought the Brits had the greatest nation," I add to tease him. I should have known better. Papa takes offence. Tatie takes advantage of his anger to provoke him further and I spend the remainder of the day paying for my mistake.

Later, when it's time for them to take their train, Tatie clings on until the last minutes. The porter signals to us with a nod of his head then a finger pointed on his watch that it's time.

"It was in this very train station that I saw you for the first time forty-five years ago," she says. "You were arriving from the airport after your flight from Canada. You gave me the book."

"*Fables and Tales.*"

Papa shakes his head at me. "You wouldn't let it out of your hands from the moment we left Québec City until you presented it to her here in the station."

I was five at the time. Papa had told me about a woman in France. I assumed I was on a journey to meet my mother. Tatie held out her arms. I ran towards her to give her the book. It didn't take long to realize she wasn't my mother. "I wonder whatever happened to it."

"I still have it," she says. "I'll take care of it for you."

I bend over to kiss her. Papa kisses me on each cheek. The porter ushers them onto the train. Papa holds Tatie's arm to help her up the steps. She turns to wave. I lose sight of them then they reappear on the other side of a dirty window. The train jerks forward. Tatie alternates between waving and wiping her eyes. The train picks up speed. I wave until I can't see them anymore.

The taxi brings me to my dingy, squatty hotel room where I fall asleep shortly after dark. During the intermittent periods of sleep, I dream that I'm in a train station filled with double-decker buses. Tatie is carrying heavy suitcases. I try to lift them. I pull harder and harder until they break open. Books fly out then turn into butterflies. They swarm us, swoop over Tatie then transform into wasps. When I move to protect her, they head towards me.

Loud voices in the room next door save me from a million wasps. The voices compete with impatient car horns and squeaking brakes from the street. It's too noisy to sleep so I alternate between bouts of reading or lying in the dark with my eyes open. I follow excerpts of conversations from the corridor and play at guessing what the language is. In the morning, someone calls from the hotel lobby to wake me. I rush downstairs and apologize to the taxi driver for being late. I feel like pre-dawn Paris, more asleep than awake. The driver asks me which terminal.

"Orly 2 to London."

He glances at me through the rear-view mirror. "You make a life in London?"

"Newfoundland."

"Finland?" he says.

An Imperfect Librarian

I switch to the French name. "Terre-Neuve, Canada."

"Canada! Beautiful nature. So cold. Snow, mountains, big cars, houses of ice."

I lean forward in my seat. "We don't live in igloos. It's cold often but you get used to the weather. Newfoundland summers are the best anywhere. Where are you from?"

"I come to Belgium two years now. Paris last year. My family come from eastern Congo. Zaire. Refugee camp. You know Zaire?"

"Only from reading *TinTin in the Congo*. You're far from home. You miss it?"

"No miss camp. I start home in this country. You have home?" He reminds me of the last line I read in Defoe's *Crusoe* before I fell asleep in the hotel:

> *Now, I look back upon my desolate island as the most pleasant place in the world, and all the happiness my heart can wish for is to be there again.*

CHAPTER THIRTY-EIGHT

'twas brillig in the slithy cove

"IF WE CAN'T LAND IN St. John's," the captain says, "we'll go on to Halifax."

I don't care if there's thirty-two centimetres of fresh snow on the ground or that gusts are in the fifty-kilometre range. The minus five degree temperatures shouldn't stop a plane from landing either. We pass through turbulence. Pressure builds in my ears. The plane drops then rises again. "Looks like we're going to have to abort the landing," the man in the seat in front of me says. A baby starts crying. The woman next to me grips the armrest. There's a jolt, a bounce then the brakes screech while the plane slows down on the runway.

The airport is swarming with throngs of stranded passengers. On my way to the taxi stand, I pass a young man lying on the floor on top of a sleeping bag. Outside the terminal, a man holding a clipboard asks me where I'm heading.

"Cliffhead, near Cape Spear."

He points to the first taxi in the line. I open the door then slide my laptop and backpack along the back seat. The interior smells of stale cigarette smoke. The seatbelt doesn't work.

"How long you here for?" the driver says.

I talk over the noise of the radio. "For as long as people will have me."

He laughs. The snow-covered roads make for a quiet ride except when the driver slams his palm into the horn because the car up ahead is going too slowly. I slouch in the seat and close my eyes to make the time go faster. I picture the Crimson Hexagon looking pink under a white gauze of snow. I imagine being naked with her, under the covers in the peak of the house. The driver turns up the heat. The car fills with the smell of the pine freshener hanging from the rear-view mirror.

I can hear the dogs barking as soon as we stop in front of the barn. The path to her house is neatly shovelled in places, drifted over in others. The key is under the step where she said it would be. I open the door slowly to let one dog out at a time. Folio comes first and jumps up on me. The other two rush out from behind. They squeal and bark then hop on me.

"Calm down. Stop!" I hold them off with my backpack but they jump and knock it out of my hands. I can't fight them so I sit on the front step and let them lick my face. Octavo and Quarto hear something in the woods then dash off. Folio pokes her nose in the backpack. I pull out a purple ball I bought in a shop in Oslo. It glows in the dark and has a remote sensing device that goes at the end of a key chain. I throw it. Folio hops through the snow then tears back to me and drops it at my feet.

"Good girl. Come on in."

Norah doesn't allow the dogs beyond the porch area. I make an exception this one time for Folio. She follows me into the porch and then into the kitchen. I read the note on the table next to the open bottle of red: *Make yourself at home. Enjoy the bread. Cheese is in fridge. Will arrive between 9 & 10. We'll toast our reunion.* Folio hops up and rests her paws on the table.

"Get down. Bad dog." I take her by the collar to lead her to the porch. Just before we reach the door, she sits. I try dragging her. "Come on. Into the porch. I'm tired. Please, Folio." She licks my jeans. I let go of her collar then rub her ears. "I'm happy to see you too."

Folio is more comfortable on the warm hardwood floors in the living room than on the ceramic tile in the porch. She likes it when, every so often, I lean forward in the rocking chair to rub her belly with my foot. After two glasses of wine, and forty pages of *Alice in Wonderland*, I don't feel like rubbing anymore. I close my eyes again and hope that Norah will soon arrive. There are no sounds except for the woodstove's fan and Folio's snoring. I stop rocking and rest my feet against her warm stomach. She jerks up suddenly and digs her teeth into her fur to chase fleas then barks and runs along the hardwood floor to the porch door.

Norah said she'd be back around nine o'clock. It's only seven. I run my fingers through my hair and tuck my shirt into my trousers. I open the door but there's no sign of Norah. I call the dogs. They crowd into the porch around their food and water. I leave the three of them behind the porch door then go up to the peak. I can smell her scent off the blankets. I prop myself up with pillows and pick a book from the pile on her bedside table: *Using Images To Improve Your Memory: 100 Mnemonic Techniques.* I return the book to the pile and close my eyes. There's no commotion in any corridor, no gurgling sounds of flushing toilets from a room above me, not a peep from the wind – nothing but a faint whisper of lazy waves trickling through beach rocks before they're swallowed up by the ocean. I count the seconds between ebb and flood. I fight to stay conscious, like someone treading to stay afloat. It's cold but I'm too tired to get out of bed to close the window.

When I wake later, Norah's naked body is lying next to me.

An Imperfect Librarian

The moonlight shines in through the window and off her hair. I shiver, then curl up against her warm body. She turns round and kisses me. I reach one arm under her neck and the other around her waist to draw her close to me. Outside, the wind is forcing the snow to fall horizontally. There are no stars to watch through the star-lights. I draw the blankets over our heads and take shelter in her desire.

It's almost early morning before I fall asleep again. As usual, Norah is up before me. She operates on the dogs' schedule and they're up at sunrise. I go downstairs in my bare feet. "Bacon and eggs? Can I help with the cooking?"

"You must be tired after a long trip," she says. "Let the dogs out then have a seat."

Octavo and Quarto go outside. Folio smells my clothes then my pocket. I leave her in the porch. Before we eat, I show Norah the *Jabberwocky and other Poems by Carroll* that I bought for her in Norway. "I didn't know if you had it in your collection already. I would have bought you something more expensive or–"

"It's the thought that counts. Thank you. *Jabberwocky* and I have a long history."

I sit at the table while she fills my plate with strips of bacon. I go to the counter for a napkin. When Norah's not looking, I slide a few strips inside it then poke it in my pocket.

"You'd be surprised how many people have never heard of *Jabberwocky*," she says as she takes off her apron and sits at the table with her back to the porch door. "Sometimes they know it's a famous nonsense poem. I'm impressed if they can recite "Twas brillig and the slithy toves did gyre and gimble in the wabe.'"

"There's a movie by that name isn't there?"

"That's *Jumanji*, not *Jabberwocky*." She passes me the salt and pepper. "In third or fourth grade, I promised some kids I'd give them five dollars if they could tell me what *Jabberwocky* was. That was a fortune in those days. When they couldn't, I said, 'You'll never be any good except to fish.' Some of them cried. Their parents warned them not to play with me. They'd chant rhymes about me: 'Yer fadder's a queer, yer mudder's a whore and you're the runt yer parents bore.' I invented my own rhymes: 'Burn your books and rot your brain. Leave the school, learn in the lane. Less you know, less you miss. Need know nuddin in order to fish.'"

I look down at my pants and see the grease stain from the bacon seeping out through the napkin. Folio watches us through the glass door. I wink at her. After we finish eating, while Norah is in the basement doing the laundry, I open the porch door to give the bacon to Folio. She rushes over to the table before I can stop her.

"Come here you little imp." I kneel on the floor then reach under the table for her collar. She sniffs my pocket. I take out the bacon and feed it to her.

"Carl!" Norah shouts.

I straighten up with a start. My head hits the underside of the table. "Sorry, Norah. Folio! Come out of there."

"I asked you not to let the dogs in the house. I told you not to feed them table scraps. Can you get the dog out of there while I go make the bed, please?"

"I said I'm sorry."

"What good is sorry when the damage is done?" she says as Folio licks the last traces of bacon off my fingers.

CHAPTER THIRTY-NINE

man, the imperfect librarian

NOT MUCH HAPPENED AT THE library while I was away except that Margaret left a message in my voicemail. She wants to schedule an appointment for me with the Chief once the privacy policy is approved. I tell Henry about the message.

"It's only a matter of time now."

"What were you saying about a miracle?"

"Enter that Crimson Hexagon, fetch me some evidence and I'll deliver your miracle on a platter," he says. "I bet you Francis is stashing Special Collections materials in there."

"You're so keen, why don't you do it?"

"I'm not the one who has to worry about Francis. In no time I'll be far away from him, far from this library. Four years, two months, one week and two days to be exact. I'll be retired, and if all goes well, sitting behind the desk in my bookstore."

"And you scold me for counting?"

"Are you any good with accounting?" he asks.

"You don't need to be good at accounting anymore. There

are very sophisticated computer programs that will do it for you."

"I'll have better things to do than counting, accounting or computing. When I'm not tending to the business, I'll be busy with writing. Did you know I have a brilliant idea for a play already? The main character is modelled after you. It's called *The Imperfect Librarian*. 'Man, the imperfect librarian may be the product of chance or of malevolent demiurgi.'"

CARL: What's that supposed to mean?

HENRY: Ask Borges.

CARL: Did you have in mind a tragedy or a comedy?

HENRY: Only high drama could capture the severity of evil gods. This nonsense with Elsa could lend it a melodramatic character. There'll need to be an element of comedy, otherwise it wouldn't be true to your character. I want to give it a Borgesian quality. I wonder if I could pull that off in a one-minute play with six scenes of an equal ten seconds each.

CARL: Or ten scenes of six seconds each or three scenes of twenty minutes each or–

HENRY: How do you say the word *enough* in Spanish and Italian?

CARL: *Basta.*

HENRY: Again, three times in a row.

CARL: *Basta, Basta, Basta.*

HENRY: Let that be a lesson for you the next time you get carried away with arithmetic.

CARL: It's not arithmetic, it's–

HENRY: I could always do some acting on the side. You've never seen my Borges' recital have you?

[Henry pauses, passes coffee mug to Carl, rises out of his seat, turns to face Carl, legs astride, ready to pounce, hand in the air, head cocked to the side staring up at hand.]

...the sky turned the rosy color of a leopard's
gums. Smoke began to rust the metallic nights.
And then came the panicked flight of the animals.
And the events of several centuries before were
repeated...With relief, with humiliation, with terror,
he understood that he, too, was all appearance, that
someone else was dreaming him.

[Henry lowers arm.]

CARL: I don't know if you're worse as an actor or a playwright.
HENRY: What do you expect with Carl Brunet for an audience? Since when did you read Borges? You thought his name meant soup the first time I mentioned it.
CARL: You're making that up. I know the difference between Borscht and Borges.
HENRY: How about *An Imperfect Librarian: The musical*?
CARL: Wouldn't be a hit.
HENRY: How about *BiblioBrunet* or *BiblioBlunder*? Or we could scrap the alliteration and settle on *Bibliofiasco*. What's your take on it? You're the central character in the production after all.
CARL: I'd prefer a more nuanced character.
HENRY: Not possible. Not among the company you keep.
CARL: What I mean is that supposing my mother hadn't given me up at birth and I didn't have to be

raised by a pair of squabbling twins?

HENRY: Then you'd have no excuse for how you are.

CARL: Imperfect?

HENRY: With an upper case I. If we weren't imperfect, we'd be gods.

CARL: I'm relieved to learn I'm no different than anyone else.

HENRY: Don't jump to conclusions.

CARL: Maybe I'm the one who's perfect and everyone around me is imperfect.

HENRY: Delusional is more like it.

CARL: What's the cure?

HENRY: No cure for the delusion. As for the imperfection, get out more, feast your eyes on the lasses.

CARL: Not everybody is as horny as you are.

HENRY: What do you understand about horny besides toads? Passion. Imagination. That's what makes being imperfect worthwhile.

CARL: I'd prefer to make it disappear.

HENRY: Start by reading a book. You're surrounded by them and you don't even read.

CARL: I probably read more in the first twenty years of my life than most people do in a lifetime.

HENRY: You'd never say.

CARL: Where do you fit on the scale of imperfection?

HENRY: I'm part of a minute minority of superior, all-seeing, all-knowing beings. If you hang around me, who knows? Some of the perfection might rub off on you.

CARL: Will I end up with a belly like yours?

HENRY: Wouldn't hurt you to have a few bulges on your skeleton. While you're at it, find yourself a better set of binoculars, move out of the hole under Gower Street, listen to the mirror's advice once in a while, eat something besides your nails, push Francis out of your way.

CARL: Is that all?

HENRY: Grow a prick while you're at it.

CARL: And then what?

HENRY: Take your mind off your worries by aiming at something.

[They stare ahead. A ray of sunshine cuts through the stained-glass windows into the Room before them like the curtain rising in a dark theatre to reveal the stage.]

CHAPTER FORTY

yellow snow

I T'S HARD TO IGNORE THE season of silver bells and jingle bells, drummer boys, turtle doves and pear-treed partridges, especially when there's a giant synthetic Christmas tree in the centre of the Reading Room. What used to be an oasis in the middle of the library is now a forest. The tree changes our view slightly. It does nothing for our conversation. "Have you been inside the hexagon, Carl?" Henry asks. "What are you going to do about Francis?"

There's little sign of Christmas at Cliffhead. "I celebrate it every four or five years," Norah says. "I have enough to do without wasting my time decorating." The snow and cold temperatures came faster than she expected. She's behind in her chores. The rectangular bales of hay for the horses have to be stacked in the barn's loft. Normally, Walter takes care of that job but he left on short notice to go around the bay for a few weeks to take care of a family emergency. The water levels in her well are low.

"I knew I'd end up paying for all those hot summer days without rain," she says.

On the weekend, we drive back and forth to a stream up the road where we fill containers then bring them back to her house. The chores are not her only problem.

"I can lend you money for the vet bills," I tell her. "And for the roof repairs. I don't mind contributing."

"I don't want to talk about it," she says.

We're shovelling the path from her house to the barn, then to the Crimson Hexagon.

"Why is the path to the hexagon shovelled if it's not in use?"

She doesn't stop shovelling to answer my question. "Ask Francis," she says.

I stand the shovel in the snow then lean on it. "Do you have a key?"

"Hanging in the porch in case of an emergency."

"Why don't we go inside and have a look?"

"Why don't we have lunch?"

We finish shovelling the path then store the shovels inside the barn. She rounds up the dogs and we return to the house.

"What's it like inside?"

She pokes her head inside the fridge, pulls out leftovers then lays them on the table. "Small, six sides, two stories, open concept, filled with boxes. I haven't been in there in ages. Will didn't include me in his projects. I explained that to you more than once already."

I add wood to the stove then join her at the table. "What's in the boxes?"

She fills my plate with salad and quiche then pours me a glass of white wine. "Books, more books, papers. Will's papers."

"Would I be able to have a visit?"

"Ask Francis."

"You know as well as I do that's not possible."

"Why? He won't bite you," she says.

"He's always interfering in my work."

"I thought it was the other way round."

"How can you say that when he's set up an entire committee to fight my project?"

"The committee is fighting for privacy rights," she says.

I lay down my fork and knife. "Are you agreeing with him?"

This time, she's the one who stops eating. "What if I was?"

"Then I'd say you need to reconsider whose side you're on."

She pushes her plate away and stands up from the table. "I'm going for a walk in the cove before this turns into one of those arguments."

I follow her to the porch. "Those arguments?"

She pulls on her boots and a jacket. "The ones that start with your questions about Francis. The last time we had an argument like that, we didn't see each other for a couple of months."

"We haven't finished lunch and we just came inside."

"I told you before I'm not interested in talking about Francis."

I put on my boots and jacket. "Why?"

She opens the door. The wind rushes in. The dogs rush out. She follows them. "I'm not interested in talking about this." She shouts to me over the noise of their barking. "It's simple."

I run after her. "It's not so simple."

She walks on ahead of me on the narrow path. "Why?" she asks.

Our conversation is being swallowed up by the howl of the wind, the barking dogs and the roar of the surf. I lay a hand on her shoulder to stop her from walking away.

"Because people have to protect themselves, that's why. Let's go back to the house and finish lunch."

"Protect themselves against what?" she asks.

I draw her close to me. She rests her head on my chest. I bend my head to kiss her. "Against the cold. Come on."

Folio jumps on me. Octavo jumps on Folio. Quarto jumps on Octavo. We fall like dominos into a fresh drift of snow. The dogs bounce up and down, trampoline style. I cover my face while they stir up a miniature blizzard. The oversized crystals of snow fall so slowly I wonder if they shouldn't be going up rather than down. I can't tell where the sky begins and the land ends. I lick the snowflakes off her cheeks. She holds a snowball up to my mouth. I take a bite then spit it out because it tastes bitter. She laughs.

CHAPTER FORTY-ONE

the honest thief

"**I**'M GOING TO THE OFFICE to pick up student papers," she says. "I'll be home in a couple of hours. Don't let the dogs inside while I'm gone, please."

I wave goodbye from the door. On the wall, next to where my hand rests, is the rack of keys. I go back to the kitchen to browse the weekend newspaper article on online music sharing. I take the scissors from the kitchen drawer to cut it out so I can post it on the bulletin board in the lunchroom at the library. The dogs are barking outside. I open the door and call to them but they don't come. My eyes shift to the key rack. Each key is labelled: *barn, Walter, basement, CH, car spare.* I put on my jacket and boots. I check my watch, look outside, then back at the keys.

The only witnesses are the dogs. The wind scatters the powdery snow over my footprints on the path behind me. I check over my shoulder before I push the key in. The click comes, I shove with my hip, the door opens. I slide the key out of the lock. It's the filing cabinets that I see first then the tables with boxes and a computer. The space is not much bigger than her living room. It's two floors as Norah said. The top storey is nothing more than a walkway around six sides of floor-to-ceiling bookshelves, half of which are empty. The walkway is bordered by a black wrought-iron railing that leads to a spiral staircase opposite where I'm standing in the doorway.

It's not a quiet space, not with the hum of an air exchanger or air conditioning unit that's beeping. The beeping changes to a shrill alarm while I'm poking my nose into a box labelled *binding materials*. I panic, grab an armful of books from the table then slam the door behind me. I run to the car and hide the books in the trunk. The alarm stops soon after I enter Norah's house. I can feel my heart pumping. I look out through the window then go back to reading the paper. It's not easy to concentrate. I expect Norah, Francis or the police to appear any minute to demand an explanation A couple of hours later, Norah's phone rings and I jump. I don't answer. I go to the porch to look through the window. Outside, there's no sign of anyone. Not long after, my cellphone vibrates in my pocket.

"Hi. It's me, Norah. Just got to the office a while ago." She pauses. "Hello? Carl?"

"Hello, I'm here, yes."

"I tried calling you on my line. I wanted to ask you to take the chicken out of the freezer. There was no answer. Where are you?"

"I'm here. I was in the bathroom when the phone rang." I was *near* the bathroom. Changing one preposition doesn't make it a lie. I may have become a thief but I'm not a liar.

The books stay in my car for the night. The next morning, I drive straight from Cliffhead to the library. I open the trunk, put the books in my briefcase then lock the car. Just before I enter the library, I change my mind. I return to the car and leave the books in the trunk. This time, I don't bother to lock it. The books are still there the following day. So are Henry's reminders. "Won't be long now before the privacy policy has its final approval," he says.

"I don't care anymore. I've given up."

"You can't give up when you haven't even begun. What are you going to do? Resign? Go back to Norway and live with your princess?"

"There are worse fates."

"Such as working under Francis," he says.

"We'll see about that."

The books are still there later that day after I finish work at the library. I leave the car unlocked on Gower Street. When I finally fall asleep that night, I dream I'm back in Norway and Elsa is holding the books in her lap. Then Francis is driving my car. We're heading down Cathedral Street. The brakes aren't working. He's cursing. When I wake, I'm sweating so much, the bed sheets are wet. I feel nauseated. I dress quickly then go to the car before I have breakfast. I open the trunk. They're still there. I put them in my briefcase and bring them back into my flat while I get ready for work.

That afternoon when Henry shows up for coffee, the four volumes are on my desk. He pats me on the back. "You're a clever man, Carl." He begins with *Newfoundland Notebooks, Dr. Cluny Macpherson*, inventor of the prototype of the gas mask. He holds one of its pages under the lamp. "There's the Special Collections stamp. See it?" he says. He does the same for the three remaining volumes. The stamps are on all of them: on the *James D. Ryan diaries (Bonavista, 1874-1919)*, on a collection of original sketches by Roger Tory Peterson called *The Birds of Newfoundland* and on *Sir William Whiteway: Correspondence and Papers*.

"Call Margaret and confirm that you'll meet with the Chief as soon as he's available." He holds one of the books in the air. "Let there be evidence!"

"Careful. Someone will hear you."

"Hear me they will and they'll hear you when you holler victory."

"Calm down, Henry."

"Now is not the time to be calm. Now's the time to be active. Put on a pot of coffee. We've plenty to do here."

"And then what?"

"We'll go home to our suppers."

"I mean what will we do with the books?"

"Not what will we do. What will *you* do?"

"Well?"

"Show the Chief the books, tell him where they came from, where they belong, make a snappy link with Francis as owner of the Crimson Hexagon, walk away with a smile on your face. Four steps."

"That's five, not four. Were you counting the smile?"

"Back off with the fucking details," he says.

CHAPTER FORTY-TWO

bibliophishing

ARGARET SAVES ME THE TROUBLE of scheduling a
meeting. "The Chief wants to see you before Christmas
holidays," she says when she calls. "How about Friday,
the twenty-second? The party's at three. Are you coming?"

"To the meeting?"

"You have to come to the meeting," Margaret says. "I meant
the party. Edith will be there."

On the day of the meeting, I arrange the books neatly in my
briefcase. I arrive ten minutes early.

"He's got someone with him. Glass of eggnog while you
wait?" Margaret says.

"No thanks."

"Fruitcake?"

I shake my head.

Margaret abandons the chair behind her desk to sit next to
me. She doesn't stay there for long. The phone has to be
answered. "Who's calling this time of day?" she says. The cakes
and treats spread on the credenza need tending. "You can't

leave here today without a doggy bag. Sure you wouldn't like some eggnog? No harm in relaxing now and then. A small glass? If you don't like it, you don't have to drink it…" Her voice trails off as she leaves the room.

I watch his office door. Margaret comes back and hands me a mug. "There's lots more where that came from." She sits next to me again. I gaze at his door. She gets up to go to the credenza. If "The Little Drummer Boy" wasn't playing in the background I might be able to hear what's happening in his office.

She lays a heavy plate of fruitcake in my lap. "There's more rum in the cake than in the eggnog. And that's saying something. Let me fill that up for you. You were thirsty after all." She leaves the room again. The phone rings. She returns. "They're calling to remind us about the party. They'll leave a message if it's important." She hands me a fresh mug of eggnog. It tastes smooth.

The Chief's door opens finally. "Brunet! Merry Christmas!" he says. He gives me a slap on the back just as I'm standing. I burp. The room moves.

"Come on in." He leads the way. "You know Francis. I don't need to introduce you."

Francis nods.

The Chief gets a chair for me. "Take a seat, Carl. Let me get you something to drink." He calls to Margaret.

Francis and I sit side by side facing the Chief's desk. Margaret didn't tell me he'd be at the meeting. I slide my foot along the floor to push my briefcase under his desk. The Chief lays a mug of eggnog in my hand. The briefcase is not at my feet. I remember that I left it in Margaret's office. I stand up. The room spins so I sit down.

"Are you going to the party this afternoon?" the Chief asks us.

Francis laughs. He moves his chair closer to mine to let the Chief get in behind his desk. "We might as well celebrate," he says. The room is too warm. My shirt is too tight around the neck.

"A toast to a new year, new projects, new alliances! Merry Christmas," the Chief says. "That's it, Carl. Drink up. Time to relax. Staying in town for the holidays?"

I nod.

"Well, here we are," he says. "And like Francis was saying, we might as well celebrate. Privacy policy's pretty much passed. First of its kind anywhere in Canada, maybe even the US. Who knows? We're very proud of our accomplishments." He raises his mug. "Here's to Francis Hickey for his dedication and diligence and–"

Francis smiles and shakes his head. "Stop."

The Chief leans back and swivels slightly, side to side in his chair. "You're sitting next to a modest man, Carl." He raises his mug to me. "Francis. Why don't you lead from here? I want to enjoy my eggnog." He calls to Margaret for refills.

"I'll get to the point," Francis says. "Most intelligent people today recognize the value of protecting personal information. They don't appreciate people spying on them virtually through a database any more than they would want someone snooping around in their office while they're not there. I'm sure, Dr. Brunet, you can appreciate the merit of these arguments."

Margaret comes back to the room with a jug of eggnog plus three plates of cake and fudge. She tops up our mugs.

"All ready for Christmas, are you, Margaret?" the Chief says.

"Thank God, the stores are open till midnight," she replies.

"Doesn't matter as long as you bought my gift." He laughs. Margaret laughs. Francis looks at his watch. Margaret leaves.

"Close the door behind you, will you?" the Chief says.

"Francis…you were saying."

"We'll need to make some changes to ensure the policy is implemented the way it should be. One of those changes involves database access and who gets to see what and why. That brings me to the point of your project. What is it called again? Bibliophishing?"

I don't bother to correct him. He knows the difference.

"I'll be back in a minute," the Chief says. "I'll have Margaret top up that jug of eggnog before she heads off to the party. Eat your cake, Brunet." He walks around the side of his desk. Francis moves his chair again. I study the back of his head, wondering how he manages to shave it so smoothly. I catch a whiff of men's cologne as he turns his head back towards me. The smell triggers a wave of nausea.

The Chief reappears. He refills our glasses then sits down with a thud. "Margaret says the party's started. They're setting up the mikes to play a few tunes," he says. "How about we move things along, Francis?"

Francis checks his watch again then turns to face me. "In a nutshell, you won't be working on your project anymore. Instead, you'll be responsible for devising systems that promote efficiency of information management within the library. Those systems will safeguard the privacy of patrons, staff and management. They'll be progressively refined to the point where they can be scaled to other units of the university such as Human Resources." He looks over at the Chief. The Chief raises his mug again. I raise mine to my lips and gulp down what's left.

"I'll be the sole person in charge," Francis adds. "We don't want too many cooks spoiling the broth, poking their noses in where they shouldn't or setting off alarms, do we, Dr. Brunet? Brunet? *Brunet!* BRUNET!!!"

The last thing I remember as I fall to the floor is the expression on Francis' face as I throw up in his lap.

CHAPTER FORTY-THREE

visiting hours

M R. MERCER SHARES HOSPITAL ROOM 2A Northeast
with me. He updates me hourly on meteorological
conditions. "We'll be snowed in till July if this
continues," he says. His television never strays from Channel 19,
the weather station. Unlike me, Mr. Mercer entertains no
visitors: no Mercedes to perform personal nursing care,
no Henry to humour, no Edith for the talk of the town, no Norah
to hold a hand. His diagnosis comes before mine: his pancreas is
under-functioning and my thyroid is over-functioning. The
doctor promises me, once they have my condition under
control, I'll be feeling like a new man: no more sleepless nights,
exhausting days or unexplained weight loss.

"Will I qualify for a new job?" I ask him. The humour goes
unappreciated.

Henry, Mercedes, Cyril and Edith are gathered around my
bed. I tell them about the prediction for the new man. Henry
predicts that my transformation will make Lazarus' resurrection
look like a mere yawn. The conversation turns to what happened

after I passed out in the meeting. Henry asks who's going to pay the dry-cleaning bill for Francis' suit. Edith and Henry laugh. "Margaret gave me your briefcase, by the way," he says. "You should have–"

Before he can finish his sentence, the door opens and Norah walks in. She sits on the side of my bed. I hold her hand. "Thanks for coming. Everyone, this is my friend Norah. You know Edith, I believe. You don't know Cyril and Mercedes, my landlords."

"Don't be calling us landlords," Mercedes says. "We're more like family, wouldn't you say, Cyril?"

"Family, yes. Carl and me are brothers and you're the mother."

Even Mr. Mercer can spare a smile in spite of the seriousness of the approaching low weather system. "Did you hear about what's on its way up the eastern seaboard?" he says. "If the winds stay nor' east, she'll be some storm. We'll be in for another thirty-five centimetres."

"I was on the phone to Dublin with my youngest lad," Henry says. "I was telling him, 'Imagine a week of steady rain squeezed into one storm. Imagine snow instead of rain.' He won't believe me. 'Go on, Da. Yer exaggeratin',' he says. Forty centimetres in December. Bring in the army. Either that or raise the white flag. Surrender now while we're still standing."

"If the power station in Baie d'Espoir is damaged in the storm, the whole city will be in the dark," Cyril says. "That's excluding Carl. They've got their own generator here at the hospital."

"He's been in the dark most of his life. Isn't that so, Carl?" Henry adds.

Mercedes frowns. "That's a sin. Poor Carl."

"I never seen the likes, not in seventy-four years and I seen plenty," Mr. Mercer says. "We had no forecasts to warn us once upon a time. No such thing as the Weather Channel. We kept an eye on the wind and the barometer. Those were the days." He sighs and drops his head onto his pillow.

Cyril bounces off Mr. Mercer's memories to tell a story about how someone in Labrador was caught chopping down an electrical pole for firewood. Mercedes bounces off that story to complain about cabin break-ins. Edith ricochets off Mercedes to talk about the cost of property insurance. Norah bounces off nothing or no one besides the silence in between.

"I need to hit the road before the drifts turn into barricades," she says not long after she arrived.

Cyril asks Norah where she lives.

She fumbles in her pockets for her keys. "In Cliffhead, near Cape Spear where there's so much snow, you can't distinguish the valleys from the hills anymore."

Norah leaves. The room is quiet.

"It's about time we met your friend," Mercedes says. "Nice looking woman, isn't she, Cyril?"

The nurse peeps around the door to announce the end of visiting hours. Henry says goodnight for everyone. "I must go chat with those lovely nurses and congratulate them on the fine job they're doing. Stay alive till tomorrow, Carl. You too, Mr. Mercer. I'll be by for another visit."

Mr. Mercer falls asleep shortly after they leave. His snoring is steady except for the gaps in between when he doesn't breathe and I wonder if I should call for a doctor or nurse to check on him. The weatherman's voice plays in the background. It's interrupted now and then by the loudspeaker in the corridor: "Paging Dr. Linegar. Paging Dr. Linegar. Dr. Linegar, please go to the emergency ward. Dr. Robert Linegar to emergency." When I close my eyes I can hear everything brilliantly, including pages for Linegar, Mr. Mercer's snoring, not to mention ice pellets hitting the window. The cacophony plays on like a raucous marching band until the nurse prescribes earplugs and a sleeping pill.

An Imperfect Librarian

Early the next morning, they wheel me off for tests. The real test comes when they bring me back to the room. "Your wife called the main desk and your girlfriend visited," Mr. Mercer says. "Too bad you weren't here when she was describin' the storm surge. The size of the waves! Right up to her window, she said. She left you some bread and jam there. She brought me some statistics from the Internet. Marvellous source of information. Ever used it?"

It doesn't take much to piece together the details of what happened. Tatie contacts Elsa to tell her I'm hospitalized. Meanwhile, Norah comes for a visit but I'm not in the room so she goes to the nursing station. A nurse asks her if she's my wife. The other nurse interrupts to say she already received a long distance message from Mr. Brunet's wife in Norway.

I leave messages on Norah's phone at work and home. "What happened today at the hospital was a mistake. In fifty-three days, I'll be divorced. Call or come see me." Later that day when I call again, she answers. There's a trivial exchange of questions about my health, a description of damage caused by the storm surge at Cliffhead, then Norah lets loose with her own surge. "You've made things far more complicated than they needed to be. I don't want to say more. I'm at work. You're not well. I'll come by later."

I call her name. In reply, I hear the monotone hum of a disconnected line.

CHAPTER FORTY-FOUR

timbit fairies

I'LL SOON NEED A SPREADSHEET to manage my list of should haves: SH told Norah about Elsa; SH divorced Elsa ages ago; SneverH married Elsa. Henry arrives for a visit and I'm in a SH mood. He sits on the edge of the bed even though there's a chair for visitors. He brings me a double espresso and a box of Tim Hortons Timbits. One by one, he pops the small round donuts into his mouth and sucks on them like they were sugarplums.

"Listen, about Norah. I know you advised me to stay away from her but I think she's good for me."

"Drink Guinness if you want something good for you. The woman is mixed up with Francis," he says.

"It's more complicated."

"No kidding."

Mr. Mercer isn't wearing headphones. Nor is the nurse who comes by to update my chart. Henry follows her around the room like he was tied to her with a string. She checks my blood pressure and temperature then leaves. Henry sits on the bed again. "They're saying kinder things about you now: 'We worked him too hard.' I laughed at that one. 'Nobody made him feel welcome.' Josephine from binding said that. She must have forgotten about my efforts, right, Mr. Brunet?"

"Surely, yes, Mr. Kelly."

He hops off the bed, pops another Timbit in his mouth then looks in the drawer of my bed table. "If you change your mind about going after Francis, you've only to say the word." He walks over to Mr. Mercer's bed. "How are you today? Heart still beating? How's that storm progressing?" He helps him with his pillows then adjusts the arm of the suspended television set.

"Where's it gonna end?" Mr. Mercer says. "One good thing: it's keepin' the weather forecasters busy, that's for sure. The Weather Channel'd have nothin' to report if it wasn't for Newfoundland. They'd have poor ratings without us."

"Well, you and Carl have plenty to keep your mind off the weather with those healthy, young nurses dancing around your bedside like sugarplum fairies. By the way, Carl, Mercedes offered to introduce me to her friend Nancy. We're going to dinner on Saturday. Nancy's another woman you've been hiding from me. Mr. Mercer, you're sharing a hospital room with a real Casanova. Did you not hear him reciting: Elsa, Edith, Norah or Nancy. I've so many, I'll pick my fancy."

"Thanks, Henry. The only thing Casanova and I have in common is that he was a librarian."

He plops another Timbit in his mouth, sits on my bed again and bounces. "What's she like?"

I move to the side in my bed to give him more room. "Norah?"

He bounces again. "Nancy," he says. "Any cleavage?"

"I've only met her two or three times."

He gazes out through the window. "Cleavage or no cleavage, I can't wait. We're heading to the steakhouse. I love a thick, juicy steak, medium rare, mashed potatoes on the side, gravy. I wonder if I could lose a few pounds by then."

"In three days? Not unless you sever a few limbs."

"Not what I had in mind," he says.

"If you wore a longer shirt, you might look slimmer."

He lifts his shirt then leans over to look for his navel.

"It's there. Big, round, visible every time you wear that shirt," I reassure him.

"It drives the women wild," he says.

I nod to confirm then raise my eyebrows for added effect. "I bet."

"My cardiologist said it was the cutest one she's ever seen."

"I didn't know you had a heart problem."

"I don't. What I have is a beauty for a cardiologist. I call her every so often: 'Dr. Hogan, I can feel my heart skipping. I think this is it.' 'Come over right away,' she says. I take off my shirt and lie down. She bends over me with her stethoscope and my heart pounds at the rate of a jackhammer gone berserk because I'm gazing straight down that long, narrow crease between her melons."

"Buy a shirt if you don't own one."

He squints at me. "Right you are. Easier than dieting. You are getting better. Giving me advice for a change. Whoever would have thought?" Henry cuts short his visit to take a detour to the shopping mall for a new shirt.

Not long after, Edith arrives with a box of Christmas decorations. "Continue on with whatever you were doing. Don't worry about me. I'll keep myself busy." She turns on her portable CD player with Christmas music.

I go back to working on my laptop. When Edith's finished decorating, I call her over by my bedside. "Do me a favour? Pick me up a gift for Mr. Mercer? A Christmas gift?" I whisper.

"I'd be happy to play your Christmas elf. What did you have in mind?"

"A book about the weather, storms, lots of pictures, colour. Don't worry about the cost."

"Anything else?"

"If I wasn't stuck in the hospital, I might have bought you a book. What would you have liked?"

"Nothing at all for me."

"Don't you have a favourite book or author?"

"I like to read for the sake of reading."

"What if everyone had to memorize one book to be communicated to future generations, what would yours be?"

"That's a strange question."

"Just curious. I was thinking about *Fahrenheit 451* lately and people learning books off by heart."

"Why didn't you say so in the first place? Under the circumstances, we'd need to preserve the great literature of the world. Shakespeare. *Romeo and Juliet*. Definitely. The greatest love story of all time."

"I'd like to buy you a fine copy for Christmas. Can you look for one?"

"If you'll autograph it: *to my Juliet*."

"How about we settle on: *Merry Christmas from your good friend Carl*?"

Edith's visit ends. Then comes the prodding and poking by the doctor, a visit from the nurse, an inedible hospital supper, and finally, a visit from Norah. I ask her to draw the curtains around my bed but she plays coy. She complains about the state of the road and hints that she'll need to leave early.

"You only just got here. I want to be with you."

She kisses me on the forehead. "Sometimes, Carl, you're so much fun to be with. I have wonderful memories of the summer we spent together, like the time the oar fell in the water. You jumped in after it with your life jacket and Folio thought you were drowning. Other times…"

"Other times what?"

"Other times you complicate things unnecessarily."

"I'm going to be divorced soon. I haven't been with her, with Elsa, in ages."

She lowers her head. "I'm not talking about that. I'm tired. Really I am. They didn't give me tenure. They said I wasn't doing enough research."

I reach forward to wipe off a tear from her cheek. She turns away from me. We hold hands in the blinking lights of the uninvited Christmas tree. The conversation shifts to the weather, the animals and her planned visit to Walter's family for Christmas dinner. She leaves when the nurse arrives.

Mercedes, Cyril, Henry and Edith show up early the next morning. Henry sits on Mr. Mercer's bed. They finger through the weather book and exchange weather stories. Henry opens the Swiss chocolate bar. "Eighty percent cocoa. I wasn't skimpy on your gift, Carl, was I?" he says.

Cyril and Mercedes give me a book on hockey. Cyril explains the new rules the NHL wants to bring in and why they could favour the Canadiens over the rival Leafs. Mercedes and Edith concentrate on the Scrabble game. That's a gift from Edith. The St. Bonaventure's College school choir is doing rounds of rooms. They sing "We wish you a Merry Christmas."

I wish. But I don't waste it on a Merry Christmas.

CHAPTER FORTY-FIVE

a knight in aluminium armour

TRUE TO THE PREDICTIONS OF my doctor, I emerge from the hospital a new man. Wish I could say as much good about my car. While I was in hospital, it was buried under a mountain of snow – most of it dumped by the plough. Cyril said it took two men to shovel it out. He had a peek at the engine then replaced the battery for me. He won't take any money for it. "In exchange, you can let me win at the next game of 120s," he says. I'm willing to forgive its squeaks and squeals on condition it can get me to Cliffhead. It starts OK. In the end, the problem's more with the road than the car. No one ever taught me to drive on an obstacle course with drifts that behave like speed bumps, patches of black ice slick as grease under the wheels or occasional white-outs that make me wonder if I'll still be on the road when they pass.

Her private road is ploughed better than the main. The dogs bark when I pull in near the barn. They run to the car. "No, Folio! Get down, Folio!" Norah's not as enthusiastic with her welcome. She doesn't bother to stop shovelling the walkway to greet me. She doesn't stroke my head or draw me closer. We don't lie together hugging in the snow. There's no talk of missing each other, no smell of her hair.

I follow her into the porch. There are muffins bottom-up on a rack on the kitchen counter. There's the usual faint whiff of wood burning in the stove. The kitchen light is a quiet copper glow from the orange and red glass in the tiffany lamp over the table. Straight ahead, in the living room, there's the natural light of day, the kind Mercedes claims is best for cleaning and dusting. Back in the kitchen, Norah finds ways to be busy.

I lay my jacket over the arm of the chair then glance at the spiral bound manual: *Faculty Association Grievance Procedures.* She clears off the table.

"How have you been?"

She places a mug in front of me. "OK."

I take hold of her hand but she pulls it away. "Elsa and I are not what you think. I never talked about it because it didn't matter because you know how I feel about you."

She goes to the counter and starts washing muffin pans. "Why were you watching me in the Reading Room?"

I was prepared for a question about Elsa. "I can't help it if my office looks down into that space."

"You'll only make this conversation more painful by denying it," she says.

The coffee pot gurgles.

"I'm not denying anything. It's not what you think. Henry had a plan to save my project and–"

"I asked *why you* were watching me, not why your friend Henry was watching."

"I told him I didn't want to use binoculars–"

"Oh my God. I don't believe you." She picks up the cloth to wash the counter.

"It didn't last for long. I didn't want to do it but he–"

"You also asked a clerk in the Reading Room if you could see my request slip. Are you going to blame that on Henry as well?"

"I just wanted to check in the databases to see who you were because–"

She lays down the cloth, opens a drawer then takes out an envelope. "Binoculars? Database? Plus snooping in Francis' office, telling the Chief Librarian that Francis was linked with my father in some scheme to rob the library, talking–"

"That's not true! Francis is feeding you lies. You can't believe anything he says."

She reaches her hand into the envelope then throws five photos onto the table. I wonder if they cost her as much as I paid for them. No wonder the cook said business was booming. "Why should my relationship with Francis concern you? I don't interfere with your life."

I shove the photos away from me. "The cook was Henry's idea. Besides, you can interfere as much as you want. At least then I'd have some reassurance you care about me."

She pushes them back towards me. "Is that how you show you care? And this too?" She throws another photo on the table. It's a slightly unfocused shot of a man in the entrance to the Crimson Hexagon, wide-eyed like an animal caught in headlights. I feel like I'm in a hole so deep, I'd need an elevator to get out of it.

"Francis gave me the photos while you were in hospital. I didn't mention them at the time because you weren't well."

"Francis is the one who's unwell."

"What's wrong with you? What have you got against him? He's a good man."

"He's a good liar and a good manipulator. I can see he's manipulated you."

"Your liar gave up a scholarship to Princeton because Will

needed him here to work on his collection of Newfoundland materials. Your manipulator was more caring to me than my own father."

"If he's such a knight in shining armour, why aren't you with him now?"

"Why aren't you with your wife?"

"Because I don't love her."

"I couldn't force Francis to love me."

"You'd have to be an idiot to love him."

"Are you calling me an idiot?"

"That's not what I meant."

"Stop interfering. Leave Francis alone!"

"If you're foolish enough to care about Francis, you deserve what you get."

She shakes her head. "Who appointed you judge of what I deserve? How dare you, of all people, pretend to know what I need? Francis was right about you."

"Meaning?"

"He told me you were spying on me." She pauses. "He told me there was a librarian watching, checking on me. I didn't believe him. Who could be that anal to want to spy on other people?"

"Is that to get me back for the comment about being an idiot?"

"It's to show you that I couldn't believe you'd be so preoccupied with someone else's affairs. It's none of your business what I was doing in that room. If I want to take my father's materials that's my business. If Francis wants to help me that's our business. None of it has anything to do with you."

"It's about time you admitted you're involved with him."

She pounds her fist on the counter. "I'm not admitting anything. What we were doing is none of your business."

"That's where you're wrong."

She turns her back to me and faces the sink. "I never should have bothered with you. I shouldn't have even approached you at the booth that day. I was only doing it to prove to Francis that you were harm–"

"You were using me."

She picks up the cloth and scrubs the counter again. "I was defending myself. I didn't know who you were, beyond some computer technician who–"

"I'm a librarian. Don't you realize that by now? You were dishonest from the beginning, all the way throughout."

"It's ironic you interpret it that way. My perspective is the exact opposite."

"So it's my fault. Is that it?"

"If you hadn't interfered–"

I stand up from the table. "If I hadn't interfered, we may never have met each other."

"Perhaps that would have been better," she says.

The sentence has the clarity I've been expecting and dreading at the same time. "Goodbye, Norah. Thanks for everything. Lessons, meals, bonfires."

She throws the cloth in the sink. The counter sighs relief. She goes to the living room then up the stairs to the peak. I take a last glance across the stretch of hardwood floor to the windows. I open the door to the porch. Folio is waiting for me. She has no photos to throw in my face or surprise revelations that make my stomach churn. I pat her head and rub her ears. She licks my hand. "That's enough now. Stop that. Don't jump up. Folio. No!" I squeeze out through the door backwards. I hold her off with my hand. She takes one last lick.

In the rear-view mirror I see the red of the hexagon, the same one in the photo she threw on the table. I turn off of Norah's road onto the two-lane highway. Something small and fast darts in front of me. I slam on the brakes. The car twirls around. I turn the wheel and the car spins in the opposite direction then stops with a thud against the pile of snow on the side of the road. Octavo and Quarto run out of the woods, across the road, then back into the woods again, chasing whatever it was that almost caused me to end up in a ditch. A man knocks on my window.

"You OK, buddy? Need some help?" he says.

I roll down the window. He stares in at me.

"I'm OK. It's the dogs from the lane to Cliffhead. They were chasing something. I saw it, braked, lost control."

"That's Myrick's hounds. She's wild as they are, talkin' to herself like that all the time, livin' by herself in the woods over the cliff. If somethin' like that runs out in front of you, keep on drivin'. Run it over if you got to. Don't kill yourself for a cat, fox or rabbit."

CHAPTER FORTY-SIX

happy valentine's, goddess

S O MUCH FOR MODERN MEDICINE. The new man reverts to feeling like the old man after a few weeks into the new year. Mercedes and Cyril lend me their daughter's room while Cyril finishes renovations in the basement. "You'll be more comfortable in her room," Mercedes says. Comfortable in pink? Pink carpet, bedspread, furniture, wallpaper and curtains. Sometimes, in my pink dreams, Norah loves me. I wake in the deepest pink of the night and remember the conversation at her house then bury my head in the pink pillow. On Monday, I miss her. Tuesday and Wednesday, I blame her. Thursday, I wish I'd never met her. "Perhaps that would have been better," she said.

When Cyril finishes installing the electric baseboard heaters, I move back to my flat. "You can leave the heat on blast 24/7 now," he says. The fly on the ceiling appreciates the change. I haven't seen him as active since the summer. The spider is tricked into thinking there's been a change in season and gives birth to a ball of eggs. The earwigs pack up camp to migrate to damper climes.

"By the time I'm finished with the repairs and additions, you won't be wanting a new place," Cyril says.

The heater in the bathroom doesn't trip the breaker any more and I could swear the water is warmer in the shower.

Mercedes and Cyril invite me for a Valentine's dinner. Henry and Nancy are already there when I arrive direct from the office. We congregate in the kitchen. Mercedes pushes past me to access the stove, past Cyril for the sink, past Nancy and Henry for the fridge. The two lovers are glued together. You'd think they needed to be that close to stay warm. She's taller so her arm falls down over Henry. His arm is around her waist. He told me already that they were an ideal match height-wise because, when he faces her, his eyes are at her cleavage. On the counter next to me is a vase with two-dozen red roses. The card says, *Happy Valentine's, Goddess. Love, Henry.*

Mercedes singles me out. "Where's Norah?"

"She couldn't be here tonight, unfortunately."

"More turkey for us," Henry says.

"There'll be no turkey for anyone if you don't move out of the kitchen," Mercedes says.

"Where's the powder room?" Nancy asks.

Henry and I move to the living room. Cyril stays in the kitchen to help Mercedes.

"She'd be here with you if it wasn't for Francis," Henry says. "You can blame it all on him. It wasn't enough that he tried to take your job out from under you. He took your woman as well."

"He was with her long before I came along."

"Defending him, are you now? You really are a fool."

"What do you expect me to do?"

"I expect you to stop moping around like an invalid. Prove your integrity. Expose Francis for what he is – a self-serving, arrogant, incompetent, power hungry, loud-mouth cock–"

Nancy returns from the powder room, Henry returns his arm to her waist, Cyril returns with an ale and the conversation returns to rants about how City Council should be doing more to remove snow from sidewalks. Meanwhile, the invalid returns his hand to his pocket to rub two beach rocks between his fingers. Mercedes has to do a hospital shift at eleven. The guests are invited to leave early. I take the basement stairs down through the furnace room, past the broom closet, under the pipes, directly to my bed. Upstairs, the toilet flushes. A door closes and a car engine revs. Mercedes is off to work. Soon after, the furnace cuts in and drowns out the sound of Cyril snoring in the living room where he probably fell asleep in front of the television. I fall asleep thinking about how we danced that night downtown and the man in the cowboy hat sang about the colour of a heartache.

CHAPTER FORTY-SEVEN

upside down moon

THE PRIVACY POLICY RECEIVES FINAL approval. The unit most affected is Digital Systems. There's a temporary freeze placed on my budget. My database access is curtailed. A committee headed by Francis is set up to oversee implementation of the policy. The committee will also monitor Digital Systems operations. In other words, I might as well be working directly under Francis. The union can't do anything for me because administration hasn't actually changed my position. They've merely reorganized the unit. Henry offers his familiar *I told you so* as well as his *Stand up to the prick*. Some days, I can barely get out of bed, let alone stand up.

I haven't talked to or seen Norah for nearly two months. That's not long enough for me to forget those six words that changed everything in the time it takes a pin-prick to burst a balloon. "Perhaps that would have been better," she said.

"If I were you," Henry says, "I'd be ready to chop off Francis' prick."

"Go for it!"

"It's your duty as a librarian to report on employee fraud. There's nothing wrong with being a whistle blower. On the contrary."

"'Take the books you found in the hexagon, Carl, show them to the Chief and let him take it from there.' Don't you think the plan is slightly simplistic? This is not some play, you know, Henry. This is my life, my job."

"Fine. Go to work for Mr. Hickey. Not much to look forward to unless you don't mind a job cleaning up shit after a dog."

"What if something goes wrong? What if Norah gets hurt?"

"The only time you have any imagination is when you're imagining the worst. The best thing you can do for Norah is get Francis out of her life. Francis is the owner of the Crimson Hexagon. She told you that. Don't be worrying for nothing."

"You said yourself the combat was unequal, that I was no match for him."

"Yes, but you have me. And you have an opportunity. Feigned retreat: it's a common warring technique. Right now, Francis is so busy congratulating himself, he doesn't see that you're sneaking up from behind."

"What if he turns around and catches me in the act?"

"I'm not a fortune teller, Carl. How do I know if and when the lightening might strike you? I'm surprised you're not written up in the *Guinness Book of World Records* for the amount of worrying you do. Trust me."

Trusting Henry is the only option left. It's either that or work for Francis. I call Margaret to schedule a meeting with the Chief as soon as he returns from his winter vacation. Henry coaches me up until the last moments before I go to his office. "Your role is to plant the seed," he says. "Nothing more. Once the police enter that hexagon, they'll find materials from the library. The administration will isolate the problem and Hickey will take the blame."

We exit my office at the same time. Henry takes the elevator. I take the stairs to the main lobby then to the Chief's office.

"Hello, Carl," he says. "How are you?" He's peering at the computer screen over the rims of his glasses. "Aren't they something?"

Vacation pictures are on the screen.

"That's the cottage we rented. The beach is on the other side of the hill. What an ideal spot. The antipodes of Newfoundland, did you know that? Halfway round the world. I miss it already. Pull up a chair. You'll see better."

"Glad you had a nice trip. I'd like to talk to you about–"

"Look at *this* one. Wait till Deidre sees them. I only downloaded them off the camera a few minutes ago. I haven't adjusted to the time change yet. Did you ever see a more beautiful sunset?"

"I need to discuss–"

"There's another sunset. No, that's not right. That's the sunrise. Sundials in the southern hemisphere have the hours in reverse, you know. The moon is upside down compared to our view. There's the aurora australis. Or was it called aurora australias?"

"I have another appointment soon."

"See how clear the sky is in this picture? There's less pollution than in the northern hemisphere. Population's not as dense, less industrialization."

"I came here today because I want to inform you of theft from Special Collections."

His eyes are glued to the screen. "That's a couple. His name was John. Now what's her name? Heather? No, that's not it. Karen? Paula? Darn!"

"I'm not talking about patrons idly stealing a book here or there. I'm talking about employee fraud."

An Imperfect Librarian

"Heather. That's it. There she is again in this picture. That's their place. A ranch. Horses. Cattle. Amazing."

"I've been thinking of going to the media or the police with this."

He draws back from the screen. "What was that?"

"I've been thinking of going to the media or the police with this."

"Have a seat, Carl."

I'm already sitting. "I'm here because I want to report on employee fraud. As you know, this sort of thing is not uncommon in libraries with rare and valuable materials like what's in Special Collections." I take out my briefcase, open it then lay the books on the desk, one next to the other. I plug the hand-held light into the wall.

"What's this about? A magic show?" he says.

I scan a page with the light to show him the stamps. "These are Special Collections materials. You know as well as I do that they're not supposed to circulate outside of the Reading Room. They were in a warehouse not far from the city. What's more intriguing is that the warehouse was willed to Francis Hickey by the late William Myrick who you know is–"

"Slow down. Where are you going with this? What do you expect me to do?"

"In the short term, someone needs to do an inventory of Special Collections. In the long term, we need a more robust, internal, computerised, security system that protects against patron theft and employee fraud. If you don't act now this could turn into a major scandal for the library and for the university in general, a media field day where you'll be eaten alive. On the other hand, we can make it appear strategic. as if, in your normal efficient process of checking on budgets, you detected inconsistencies. You contact the authorities. They'll handle the messy part. In the end, one employee will be judged guilty and one administrator will be judged in control."

He gazes off into space, calm, pensive. The hint of a smile emerges. It's the reassurance I need. When I leave the office, he's already on the telephone with the President. I congratulate myself.

I SH known better.

CHAPTER FORTY-EIGHT

the aspartame of librarians

THE CITY IS OPERATING IN slow motion. The parade of blizzards leaves roads virtually impassable and sidewalks invisible. The Weather Channel describes it as the biggest news story of the new millennium for Newfoundland. Over four hundred centimetres have fallen so far and it's not yet the end of February. Snow banks line streets and bury parking lots. Two hundred tons of salt have been spread on city streets. The roof of a local shopping centre collapses, the number of car accidents rises. People are asked to venture out only if absolutely necessary. There's talk of a potential state of emergency. The concrete vibrates with the energy of the ploughs and snow blowers. The weather tantrum buries my car in a mound of snow. I dig it out with the shovel, go indoors for a shower then come back out too late to stop the plough from burying it again. I call a cab. The news is playing in the car.

The RCMP released a bulletin today announcing
the seizure of a quantity of books and papers from a

property near the city. VOCM has learned that some of
the goods may be university property. An investigation
is ongoing. One person has been charged with
obstruction of justice as well as assault causing bodily
harm against an officer of the law. The individual was
released on bail pending a court hearing.

That afternoon, I make coffee in advance. It's not like Henry to be late. I'm relieved when I hear his knock.

"I'm so thirsty, I could suck a mop." He wipes his forehead then wobbles over to the stand. He tugs his shirt away from his body, reaches forward to pour coffee then stops to sniff under his arm. "Jesus, I'm roasted," he says. "I just came across campus from the President's office. I was prepared for the firing squad." He places his hands at his side, lowers his head and frowns. "'Henry Kelly. We find you guilty of being a luddite librarian.' How was that performance, Carl? Bet you thought I was too much of a luddite to know what a luddite is, didn't you?"

He wipes his forehead again then walks over to his chair. "I had my defence prepared and rehearsed. You wouldn't understand it because you're brainwashed, brain-dead, brain-challenged or whatever the politically correct term is this week. It was a brilliant but wasted speech. 'How are you, Mr. Kelly? Can I get you anything?' They didn't call me there to reprimand me. Exactly the opposite. The Chief recommended that the President place me in charge of inspecting the materials confiscated by the police in the Crimson Hexagon."

"Why you?"

"Are you doubting my abilities, Carl? In their wisdom, they chose the espresso, the orchid, the tango the *je ne sais quoi* of librarians."

"What does that make me?"

"The aspartame of librarians. The decaf version." He laughs, coughs then wipes his forehead.

"Have you heard the radio yet today?"

He shakes his head as if too exhausted for words.

"Francis has been charged with assault and obstruction of justice."

"I told you, you don't listen," he says. "Norah's been charged, not Francis. The reporters were here talking to Francis and the Chief. They're both speaking on behalf of the university. I should have guessed there was something between them. I always wondered whose prick–"

"Screw Francis! What about Norah?"

"They had a search warrant for every building on that property, not just for the hexagon. You can be sure Francis had a role to play in that change in our plans. The officers were under an order to remove every sheet of paper. They wore white gloves but it wasn't because they needed to be delicate. I can't blame her for fighting them off if she had the collection you described to me. In any case, her friend Walter is going to bail her out of jail."

"Is that supposed to make it better?"

"For now it might, yes."

CHAPTER FORTY-NINE

eavesdroppings

THERE'S A PERSISTENT DRONE OF rumour sounding throughout the library and on campus in general. The lunchroom is much noisier than usual.

"It's not the cameras that caught her, you know," the woman says. "It's Francis Hickey."

"He's some good lookin'," the woman next to her adds.

"Too good for me. Never go out with a guy who looks better than you–"

I push my chair in. It squeaks and interrupts the conversation.

"No worries about that happening around here," the woman says as I'm leaving the room.

VOCM, CBC, *The Campus Voice*, *The Telegram*…even the national *Globe* is reporting on the story. Francis poses with a smile. The captions reads: *Special Collections Expert Francis Hickey*. Norah's photo doesn't appear in the papers but her name is on everyone's tongue. I can't stop the newspapers or the rumours. I've sent her emails and a letter through regular snail mail. I've left telephone messages. If I tried any harder to contact her, I'd be guilty of harassment. For every email or letter I've written, there've been ten times as many drafts. I substitute words, add, delete, edit, explain, deconstruct, reconstruct. Every page ends up in the trash. The posting to the online discussion is my last resort:

> *To: king_e.group.nl.ca*
> *From: cbrunet@king.nl.ca*
> *Date: March 02, 2001*
> *Subject: Help Norah Myrick*
>
> ---
>
> *Visit ratemyprofessors.com to voice your support for*
> *Dr. Norah Myrick, Assistant Professor, History*
> *Department, King E. University. Norah needs your*
> *help now!*

Within a week, there are forty-six postings. My favourite is, *Come back Professor Myrick, we loves ya!!*

Every time the phone rings, I answer hoping it will be her. But it never is.

"Hi. Edie here. How are you?"

"OK."

"You sound sluggish. Is everything all right?"

"I'm fine, Edith. What can I do for you?"

"You're in a hurry again. I can tell. I was calling to invite you for supper."

"Not tonight, thanks."

"I didn't mean tonight. I've got toastmasters. I meant sometime on the weekend. Friday or Saturday. Curling with the girls is off for this weekend. I was going to invite another couple. Do you know Betty and Mike?"

"No."

"They're a lovely couple, about our age–"

"I meant, no I can't come for supper."

"Why not? It'll be a lovely evening. We'll play charades. Betty is excellent. She–"

"I have to go now, Edith."

"Carl, are you there? Don't hang up. I also called to see if you'd heard the news."

I don't have a TV, the car radio is broken and I'm thinking I might get rid of my phone as well.

"It's about Norah Myrick."

"What about Norah?"

"I thought you'd know by now. You two were a number this summer, weren't you? Are you still with her?"

"What about Norah?"

"She was picked up for failing the breathalyser a few years ago. Did you know that? There's nothing worse than being involved with–"

"What about Norah?"

"Everybody's heard by now. You should get yourself a TV or a radio."

"What about Norah?"

"She's missing. There's a search party out around the Cape Spear area where she lives. If you ask me, I'd say she's hiding out somewhere. Would you like to come for–"

I haven't driven over the road to Cliffhead in months. The mounds of snow are piled high. In open areas, drifts are blowing over the tops of the orange snow fences. Except for a few skidoos, SUVs and a couple of pickup trucks, I'm the only one on the road. The truck in front of me is moving so slowly you'd think it was carrying a load of gravel, not a load of firewood. They should give out tickets to people who drive at that speed. When we arrive at the hill, the driver shifts gears and the truck goes even more slowly. As soon as I get a clear stretch of road, I push the gas pedal to the floor to pass him. The driver makes one of those friendly twitches of the head as if to say give 'er. I speed on past, though not for long. He slows down to stare while I'm pulled over on the side of the road. The policeman saunters up cautiously to my car and taps on the window. "Driver's license, please."

"Do you think we could do this quickly? I'm in a hurry."

"You've had enough doing things in a hurry for one day. I had you clocked at thirty kilometres over the speed limit."

"I'm on my way to join the search party for Norah Myrick at Cliffhead."

"You're not from here, are you?" he says.

"What does that have to do with anything?"

"If you were from here, you'd know you should hand over your license, say thank you, officer, and hope that I don't take you into headquarters."

"I can't go to headquarters. I have to join the party. She's missing. You must have heard about it. You're a police officer."

"Thanks for the reminder, Mr. Brunette. Your party will have to wait. Stay there while I go to the car and plug this information into the database."

"You don't need to check with it in the database. I have an accent and drove over the speed limit. That doesn't mean I'm a criminal."

"Calm down there, mister. This is a routine check."

Sixteen and a half minutes. I could have been to Cliffhead in that time. "I guess your computer was slow today."

He doesn't react. He simply pauses and glares at me. "In the future, watch your driving, and your attitude, Mr. Brunette," he says. He saunters back to his car. I shove the speeding ticket in the glove compartment. He tailgates me until I turn off onto Norah's private road. Henry told me I should get winter tires. They wouldn't have been any use on this road. The only thing that would get through is a snowmobile or a plough. When I can't go forward anymore, I put the car in reverse. The tires spin. The back of the car starts to slide towards the ditch on the side of the road.

I turn off the engine, search for my phone then realize I left it in the office. The windshield fogs up. I open the window. A cold draft of air blows inside. I open the door and step out in my office shoes, without mitts or a scarf. I've done the walk many times alone or with her in fifteen minutes. Now, it takes twice as long and that much more energy. I run to keep warm. I hop over drifts. If she's there, I'll go inside and warm up by the woodstove.

She's not there. The entrance is smothered in snow. There are no footprints. I check around the barn. The padlock is tight on the door. There's no sign of any cars. I call the dogs. Three crows sitting on a wire watch me. I follow my prints back to the car, climb inside and turn the heater on high. It makes a squeaking sound then farts a burning rubber smell. I climb out, slam the door shut, leave it unlocked and hope someone steals it.

Once I reach the main road, I stick out my thumb. The police car that stopped me earlier drives past. I turn to face the opposite direction then raise my collar up over my neck. His car disappears over a hill. I should have flagged him down. There's no crime in being stuck in the snow with or without an accent. As I'm waving to the police car that's already too far away, a horn blows behind me. I turn around to face a rust-trimmed pickup truck pulled over on the side of the road. The passenger door squeaks open. A voice shouts, "Where ya headin'?"

I step inside. "Any place where it's warm or to a garage. Whatever is nearest."

The truck may be old but the heat works fine. Ambrose introduces himself. "Where ya from?" he says.

An Imperfect Librarian

"From town," I tell him.

"Yeah? Which part?"

"The university library."

"I know someone from the library. What's her name again? Peddigrew?"

Ambrose drops me off at the nearest garage with tow-truck service. He drives kilometres out of his way, offers me his gloves, then asks if there's anything else he can do for me. If Edith had been there, she would have said, "God luv 'im."

CHAPTER FIFTY

i torque,
you torque, we torque

ENRY SHOWS UP FIVE MINUTES early but not in the office. He's on the other side of the window, sitting in Norah's carrel, waving to me. I stand near the glass and shake my head. He turns his back to me, bows his head then swivels round and holds up a piece of paper. I can't read what he's written. I shake my head. He lays the paper on the carrel, forms circles with his thumbs and forefingers in front of his eyes to mimic the binoculars. I take them from on top of the filing cabinet, and focus on his sign: *Coffee ready?*

I drop the binoculars in the trash bin, sit at my desk then return to writing my report: *Advanced Analysis Of User Searching: Systems Design Implications.* There's a knock at the door. "Go away!" The knocking persists. I open but only two-words' worth: "I'm busy."

"Since when did you become busy?" Henry asks.

"Since I stopped listening to your advice."

"If you're too busy, then I won't tell you about the filing cabinets."

"Tell me what?"

"Are you busy or not busy?"

I move my arm out of the way. He saunters in and over to the coffee stand.

"What about the cabinets?"

He raises a hand minus the thumb. "There were four. Police property for now. As far as the Crimson Hexagon goes, there was *nada* in there, nothing belonging to the library or to Special Collections. Between the time you were inside and the police were in there, Francis must have gutted it. Her own collection of books looks legitimate. Wish I could say the same about the materials they found in the basement of her house. They were specialized cabinets designed to preserve and protect old, rare, expensive documents. Fireproof, waterproof, everything except police proof."

"What do the cabinets matter if they weren't supposed to find them in the first place? You promised me the plan wouldn't involve her."

He shakes his head at me and laughs. "I never uttered any such promise. I don't control Francis' behaviour."

"Just tell me what's going on."

He looks down into the Room while he talks. "Your lass, Norah Myrick, your Cliffhead queen, had everything catalogued: description of each page, how the pages were related, approximate dates, authors, location—"

"It belonged to her father, to William Myrick."

"According to what I've handled so far, it belongs to the archives or Special Collections."

"You said yourself that most of the library's materials deserved to be cared for by someone who'd appreciate them. You were sympathetic to Blumberg. What about Norah?"

"Sympathy is not the issue. She'll spend enough time behind bars to read every book in the prison library twice. You shouldn't have been shagging her in the first place if she's Francis' lover. I warned you not to become involved with her."

"Stop calling them lovers."

He walks away from me towards the coffee stand. "What would you prefer?" he asks. "Partners in fornication or Romeo and Juliet? You wouldn't be in this mess if you'd listened to me."

"What will it take for you to admit you're wrong – to say, 'Sorry, Carl, I made a mistake, I misled you,' to say, 'I shouldn't have asked you to watch her with the binoculars, I shouldn't have suggested spying on her with the cook?' And let's not forget the 'Go inside that Crimson Hexagon, Carl.'"

He returns to the window. "You're a free man. You had a choice to do what you wanted. I was only highlighting the range of possibilities because you couldn't imagine them for yourself."

"*Basta!*"

"Look," he says. "The Room is waking up."

"You know something else I've had enough of?"

"I'd say biscuits and coffee. You should learn to share."

"Enough listening to you accusing me of being hypnotized by the computer screen when you're hypnotized by what you see through my office window. Enough serving you coffee and cookies, cleaning up your mess. No more advice, no more making my life any more complicated than–"

"Blaming again. You're the one who loves to keep tally. How many times is it that you've blamed me? If you gave me a biscuit for each one, I'd leave here satiated for a change."

"I'm not giving you any more cookies. There's enough crumbs under your chair to feed you for a week."

"I knew you were a cheap fellow but I never imagined you'd

resort to feeding me biscuits from the floor."

"They're not biscuits! How often do I need to explain the difference?"

"How often? Do you want an exact number or merely an estimation?"

"I'm struggling to have a serious conversation yet you sabotage it every time."

"There's your other problem. You're too serious," he says.

"I have more important things to do than waste my time on conversations that go round in circles. Didn't you say you were leaving?"

"More important things to do, have you?" he says. "Like chasing after women who are unavailable?"

"I refuse to continue this conversation. I refuse to allow you to play the psychologist. I told you that before. I simply want to be left alone."

"You said, 'I told you that before' already."

"There you go again. Why do you have to twist and torque my meaning?"

"You can't use it as a verb."

"Will you stop handling my papers, jabbing at my computer keyboard. What can't you use as a verb?"

"Torque is a measure used in physics so I can't very well torque your meaning or torque anything for that matter."

"I'm not in the mood for this today, Henry."

He abandons my desk and moves over to the coffee stand. He opens the lid of the cookie container then slides a cookie into his mouth like a child stealing a sweet. He turns side on. He's wearing the longest shirt I've ever seen on him. His belt isn't even visible.

I place my hand on the doorknob. "I'm not in the mood."

Henry chews without paying attention to me. "You should try repeating yourself less."

I TORQUE, YOU TORQUE, WE TORQUE

"Some people can't understand you no matter how often you repeat things. That's why this conversation is such a waste of time."

"You're the one doing most of the gabbing. Change the subject."

I open the door to close the conversation. "Goodbye, Henry."

He looks down to his belly, swats off something from his shirt, shakes his head, then, for his parting line, says, "Bloody biscuit crumbs."

CHAPTER FIFTY-ONE

tempest in a teacup

CYRIL TELLS ME ABOUT THE Sheila's Brush that hit the city less than twenty-four hours ago. "It's the wife of St. Patrick sweeping away the last of the winter storms," he says. We travel to the pond on borrowed snowshoes. There's no sign of Norah anywhere. I hardly recognize Cliffhead in the snow. If it wasn't for the strips of orange plastic that Norah tied to the trees during the summer, Cyril and I would never be able to follow the trail.

The gulls and crows are scarce. Cyril says if you sit still with some seed on your hand, the chickadees will eat out of it because there's so little food available to them now. We don't have time to feed the birds. I want to walk across the pond to retrace the route Norah made me swim from the beaver's house to the shore. Cyril holds his arm out to stop me. "Where're you going? See there where the stream runs in, the grass by the bog with the condensation? Mercedes would have my head if she knew we were traipsing on the ice this time of year. There's nothing here anyway. Where's this meadow you were telling me about?"

My last visit to the meadow was in the fall. We were on our way back to her house from berry-picking. Norah had filled two five-pound buckets with berries. I had two ice cream containers full. We sat near the cliff's edge. She laughed at me when I accidentally threw a handful of sour partridgeberries in my mouth then chomped down on them thinking they were blueberries. There are no berries in sight now, not a peck on the virgin snow. "Don't be worrying about her," Cyril says. "She's a smart woman. She's gone off to some friend's house till it all blows over. Have faith."

In the evening, Mercedes and Cyril are holding a Paddy's Day celebration. "We're expecting you there. Nancy and Henry are coming. Wear green," Cyril tells me. I've managed to avoid Henry lately. Every day at 3:30, there's his knock on the door. I don't answer. There was a giant-size Swiss chocolate bar in my office mail slot one day. *Don't eat it all at once. HK,* the note read. I had the secretary return it to his mail slot.

He arrives wearing a plastic green leprechaun hat with a *kiss-me-I'm-Irish* button. His arm is wrapped around Nancy's waist. He grips a bottle of beer in his hand and points it in Cyril's face as he talks. I take shelter in the kitchen. Either way, I can't escape Henry. If it's not a conversation with him, it's a conversation about him.

"Nancy would have gone out with you but now she's hooked up with him," Mercedes says.

"They seem happy."

She wipes her hands in her apron, pokes her head through the kitchen door then returns to the sink to tend to the cabbage soaking in a bowl. "If they were any happier, they'd be doing it on the floor in front of us. Nancy's never been so taken by a man in all her years. I don't know what she sees in him." She lowers her head and whispers, "He's on pills to keep his blood pressure down, pills to keep his penis pressure up, he's overweight and a fine candidate for our cardio ward. Nancy can't be expected to care for him the rest of her life."

"A nurse is probably what he needs. He would never put any faith in what I have to say to him."

"You're a fine one to be preaching. You're so skinny, the wind would blow the milk out of your tea. Go on out of my kitchen. Have yourself a beer. And not one of them light ones."

I wander into the living room away from the smell of the curried lamb. Cyril and Henry are talking. Nancy's listening. The news is playing in the background.

"It's a light version of rugby," Henry says. They're comparing refereeing in hockey with football, or soccer, as Cyril calls it.

"They're some fine crowd of soccer players in St. Lawrence."

Henry agrees with Cyril then tells him how he drove to the town to see a game. Fights broke out in the stands. He says he hasn't enjoyed an English game as much as the Newfoundland version since then. Nancy listens patiently, smiling or laughing anytime Henry speaks. He turns to face her at the end of each sentence. Every so often she bends down so they can kiss.

The news report is about Y2K. "The amount of money wasted on preparing for the worst is estimated in the millions, our sources tell us…"

The local news comes on with a pretty female news reader who's as expressionless as a statue. I recognize the sign to Cape Spear. Ray Harding is talking then Norah's picture appears. I turn up the volume: "Harding spotted the snowshoe sticking out of the ice. Divers were called to the scene, where they found only a moose carcass. The investigation into Myrick's disappearance is ongoing. Police would like to remind people to stay off the ice this time of year."

Mercedes comes into the room and asks why everyone is so quiet. Cyril turns off the television then takes her by the arm into the kitchen. Nancy follows.

Henry sits by my side, crowding me on the chesterfield. He lays his arm around my shoulders. I brush his arm off and leave the room. The hallway is dark but I know the way to the basement. I lock the door from the inside. I don't bother with the light on the stairs or in my bedroom. I pull the blankets up and around my neck. I feel myself sinking, like during those last uncountable seconds before falling asleep, or like an object floating slowly to the bottom of a pond.

CHAPTER FIFTY-TWO

redeeming apologies

I MOVE MY CHAIR FROM MY desk to face the window. I picture her in the carrel, the first time I really took notice. It was a distant image, back on, out of focus even with the binoculars.

There's a knock. "Open up. It's me."

I ignore it but he keeps knocking so I open finally. He walks in, examines my desk and flicks papers around as if he's searching for something. "How are you?" Henry says.

"Not well."

He glances at the coffee pot where there's nothing brewing. "It didn't turn out how we expected."

"I'd say. Not for me, you, Norah…"

"Sure you're not leaving anyone out?"

I haven't moved from the door since I opened it for him. "If you're going to make fun of me, you might as well leave now."

Henry talks to the coffee pot. "A little humour might be exactly the remedy, under the circumstances."

"There's a time and place for everything, Henry."

"You're right."

"I'm surprised to hear you say that."

"Me too, but it's easier than admitting I was wrong," he says.

"Admitting you're wrong won't change what happened."

He walks from there to the window. "Never does."

I sit in my chair in front of the window. "I'm glad you finally believe I'm not wrong all the time."

"If you weren't wrong now and then, you wouldn't be human."

"What's to appreciate about that?"

"If we weren't human, we wouldn't need each other."

"You don't need me, Henry."

"If I had a finer accent, a rounder belly, a more sardonic wit, I wouldn't need to be grateful to Carl Brunet, of all people, for wrangling and dangling behind the scenes to unite me with a woman as divine as Nancy."

"There was no wrangling and dangling."

"You did more than anyone else has done for me since I've been here. You can't make a decent pot of coffee, you're too preoccupied with details and numbers, you don't read enough, you haven't got any sense most of the time, but who else at this library tolerates the likes of Henry Kelly with his chronic complaining, brazen manners, filthy tongue and damning advice? Not to mention that he waddles more than a duck." He laughs then coughs.

"I'm glad you believe I have a stray redeeming quality."

"At the minimum, one. Maybe one and a half. You did win an award this year, don't forget that."

"I'm surprised the cuckolded-husband award could qualify for half of a redeeming quality."

"We might be able to bend the rules under the circumstances. I'll see what I can do."

An Imperfect Librarian

"The qualities haven't done me much good."

"They have for others."

"I hope you don't mean Norah."

He waves a dismissive hand at me. "That wasn't your fault. If you'd ignored me, she might still be with you."

"It's too late now, but I appreciate the apology anyway."

"It's not an apology," he says. "It's the facts. You're the one who claims to be Cartesian. You should be able to recognize facts when you see them."

"Chalk it up as one of my imperfections." I glance over my shoulder.

He's sitting at my desk, squinting at the screen, poking at my keyboard.

"I almost forgot why I came by," he says. "It's time I started brushing up on my computer skills. You should see Nancy with the Internet. She's a whiz. Why don't you show me a few tricks?"

"I thought you despised computers and the Internet."

"Nancy says it will come in handy to have some computer skills for my bookstore. She's right. Besides, it's important to keep up with the times. Libraries are changing. Best to go with the flow. As they say, you can't hold off the deluge with a finger poked in the dyke. How about a spot of coffee and some biscuits before we begin?"

CHAPTER FIFTY-THREE

wuthering heights:
the newfoundland version

SOMETIMES, WHEN ONE OF THOSE waves of missing her swells up inside me, I hop in my new hatchback then drive out to Cliffhead. The place feels quiet without her. The windows on the house are covered with sheets of plywood. One side of the garden fence is broken down. There's no evidence of any recent bonfires on the beach. In the meadow, there's no sign of the three-legged fox, but over by the pond the beaver is still active. It feels good to revisit the pond and remember how we used to lie side by side with our toes touching on that greedy strip of sand. I miss sharing a seat with her in the rowboat. I certainly don't miss the tannic, boggy taste of pond water. I miss the fruity, earthy smell of the mini rhododendrons, the blueberry and marshberry bushes. I miss the patient call of the white-throated sparrow in the quiet of a Cliffhead afternoon. When I'm there, I like to shut my eyes and listen to the wind. I could swear there's meaning in the sounds the gusts produce, with the surrounding spruce trees for their voice box. At times, it seems excited and happy. Other times, it's tender and affectionate. Then there are those moments when the sound reminds me of a child crying for a parent. In the early morning, the crows mimic the sound but with a harsher articulation and a telling or demanding tone. The sound's never angry, even though I expect it should be.

When I told Henry about the Cliffhead wind and how it makes me think of Norah, he glanced at me from the corner of his eye and said, "Write it all down and call it *Wuthering Heights: The Newfoundland Version*." I might consider that as a project for another day. For now, I have my hands full.

Campus Voice
August 6, 2001 Report Released

The External Committee on Operations and Procedures at King Edward University Library released its report this week. Chair Edith Peddigrew told the Voice that the Committee found "gross inadequacies and numerous irregularities in the management of Special Collections."

The report's recommendations include an initiative to investigate how knowledge and information analysis can inform administrative decisions without compromising the privacy of individuals. Dr. Carl Brunet will head up the new initiative entitled Project Jabberwocky. On September 8th, Brunet will officially launch the web site "A Room with a View," which he told the Voice will provide "online, public access to Special Collections materials."

The Campus Voice will be in attendance at the launch. Pick up your copy next week to hear more on this story.

When I'm not busy with "Jabberwocky" and "A Room with a View," I'm working on my house. It's in a sheltered nook of a bay near the ocean with a road between my land and the beach. Folio seems to like it. She's been with me ever since the day I ran into Walter by the pond. I heard someone shouting at the dogs, followed the voice and came upon him as he was checking on the traps Ray had set for the birds. Walter was trying to free a crow. Octavo and Quarto were jumping up at the bird. Folio sat nearby watching the spectacle. Walter kicked Octavo away when the dog's jaws grazed the feathers of the crow, almost catching him. I asked if I could help with the dogs.

"They're on their way to the SPCA," he said.

I couldn't imagine Folio in a cage or adopted by city people and living in some suburb, so I offered to take her. Later that afternoon, I stopped by Walter's house for her bed and food.

"Wait here," he told me after he opened the door.

I stepped into the porch then watched as he put a bag of dog food and a bowl into a cardboard box. "Any news about Norah?" I asked.

He stopped what he was doing.

"I could help her, you know," I added.

He turned round holding the box then came into the porch. He unloaded the box into my arms.

"Have you seen her?"

"There's no ghosts at Cliffhead," he said as he reached an arm around me to grab a leash off the wall. He dropped it into the box before he opened the door.

I followed him outside onto the gravel path in front of his house. "Are you implying that she's dead?"

He walked casually towards a garage. Its door faced away from me.

I set down the box to open the rear of my car. "They haven't found a body," I reminded him. When he didn't respond, I

An Imperfect Librarian

shouted, "I said they haven't found her body." He disappeared into the garage. I put the box in the car then headed after him. The garage door was raised. I stood behind. In front of us, boxes were piled to the ceiling. "Why are you assuming she's dead?" Folio stood by my side then licked my hand.

Walter took a box in his arms. I could tell by the change in his gait that it was heavy. He walked towards his house then went inside. I held Folio by the collar to stop her from going after him. While he was gone, I let her loose so I could look inside the garage. I'd seen similar boxes in the Crimson Hexagon. These were sealed.

Walter came up behind me with Folio in tow. He nudged me out of the way. More like a shove.

"Answer my question, please," I said. "I'll go then. You won't see me again. I promise. Just tell me what you know! I'll say nothing about these boxes."

He turned around, stopped and glared at me. For an instant, I thought he'd kick me like he'd done with the dog. I stood my ground. "Please. I need to know if–"

"Once a fool, always a fool." He walked out of the garage and headed to his house with another box in his arms.

Folio ran alongside as I followed behind Walter. "What do you mean?"

He walked faster than I did, even with a box in his arms. "Take Folio and go on. Ya' got no business here," he said, looking back over his shoulder. "Ya' done enough damage. Leave her in peace." Folio went inside Walter's house. I waited outside. Folio appeared first, then Walter.

"I didn't mean to do her any harm," I said. "One simple misunderstanding led to another, one innocent mistake followed another. I didn't mean to–"

"Once a fool, always a fool," he repeated quickly then brushed past.

I rubbed Folio's ears to distract her so she wouldn't run off. I wanted to explain, but it was easier to change the subject. "I don't mind helping with the bail. I know it must have been a financial–"

"The man Kelly from the library, Henry Kelly, put up the bail," he said, without a glance towards me.

I let go of the dog and followed Walter. This time he closed the door and clinched the padlock. He turned around then walked past me with such determination that he nearly knocked me over.

"Thanks, then. I'll be off," I said. "Folio will be happy at–"

The house door slammed shut.

I haven't been back to Walter's since then. That was the first and last conversation between us. As for his judgement of the fool, I'm not so sure I agree with him, although I did take his advice to leave Norah in peace. That doesn't mean I've stopped longing for her or that I don't visit the pond regularly. If I run into Walter, I'll tell him I'm there for Folio's sake.

Norah would be pleased with me for taking such good care of Folio, although she'd probably scold me for spoiling her and tell me I should punish her when she pees on the carpet in the bedroom. I plan to eventually put down a hardwood floor anyway. Norah definitely wouldn't approve of Folio sleeping on my bed. The house is so big, Folio could have her own bedroom. When Cyril finishes rewiring the place, he tells me I should consider renting out rooms to tourists in the summertime. "Mainlanders would pay a fortune to spend a week around the bay in a spot like this."

I have no plans to rent out any rooms. They're reserved for Tatie and Papa's visit. After Tatie heard what happened between me and Norah, she was ready to pack her bags. Papa didn't want to leave France, but he hates staying alone in the house at Cavaillon.

An Imperfect Librarian

They're tired and disoriented by the time they arrive at the airport. On the drive to my house I tell them about the plans for the next two weeks. We'll go to Mercedes and Cyril's house for a barbeque one evening followed by a haunted hike that starts at the cathedral just across the street. Edith has booked us a boat tour to see puffins and whales. We'll drive with Henry and Nancy to Trinity for a weekend of theatre.

After we arrive at my house, I carry the suitcases up over the steps then leave them in the living room. We go outside to visit the shed that Cyril pokes around in when he comes by. We stroll over by the wharf where a dory and skiff are docked. I tell them about when Henry visits and how the fishermen assume he's from around the bay. I joke that I'll have to book him for elocution lessons. Down on the shore, we're attacked by armies of flies. It's the offal from the fish plant nearby that attracts them. Mercedes says it won't smell as bad in the winter. I can always close the windows in the summer anyway. I haven't got round to buying fly screens so it's just as well. We return to the house and sit together on the couch in the living room with glasses of warm lemonade. Tatie interrupts the ten-minute siesta to announce that she's brought a surprise for me. She kneels on the floor next to the suitcases. "Close your eyes," she says.

Papa opens a suitcase for her. I hear the clicking of the clasps.

"Open your eyes now," she says.

I grab her outstretched hand.

"Come closer. Touch, touch!"

The suitcase is filled with books. I take them out one by one. *TinTin* and *Asterix* books are on the top layer. Underneath them I find two bundles of Jules Verne's books. I finger quickly through the tightly bound pages with their black and white engravings. In the very bottom layer, she put the smaller volumes. There's *The Song of Roland, Renard, The Fables and Tales* and many others.

I stare at them, almost incredulous. "You kept them all. I don't believe it."

"I had to fight to save them. Georges complained they took up too much space in the closet, as if we had anything else to put in there. Remember? You'd say, 'Tell me the moral, Tatie, tell me the moral.' It's time, like you, that they had a home where they belong but if you don't have the room right now, I can return them to France. It's no trouble–"

All this time Papa has been sitting quietly. He jumps up suddenly out of his seat and shouts. "We're not returning with them. I'll dump them to the bottom of the sea before I'll lift one hundred and fifty kilos of books halfway around the world again."

Folio is frightened. I call her to my side. She wags her tail and settles by my legs.

Tatie takes my hand. I help her up off the floor and onto a seat on the couch next to me.

"It's the Atlantic Ocean, not the Atlantic Sea. It's twenty-five kilos for each suitcase. Furthermore, it's not halfway round the world, it's only a quarter. Your Papa never listened to me when I used to tell him, 'Learn your lessons, Georges.'"

I can see it coming from Papa. He won't let a comment like that past him. "Why should I have listened to you?" he says. "You were always pretending to be my mother. You weren't my mother any more than you were his, isn't that so, Carl?"

Tatie holds a delicate hand to my face. I rest my head in her palm and close my eyes. There's no harshness in the touch, no solicitation or admonishment. I open my eyes again then take her hand in my own. "Of course she's my mother."

Tatie leans forward and kisses me on the cheek. "Of course."

Papa throws his arms in the air. "Why are you speaking English? That's enough, don't you think? If it continues I'll be heading home sooner than planned."

Tatie slides a tissue out from her sleeve. She wipes her eyes and nose then says the very word I had on the tip of my tongue. "Promise?"

EPILOGUE

ENRY CLAIMS IF IT WASN'T for him I'd have a permanent curve in my back from bowing to Francis. He also says I'd have a brown tongue. He still comes by in the afternoon for coffee, although not as often. I vacated the office not long after I moved out of Mercedes and Cyril's basement. "View's no better than the LAB's," he says in comparison to the Reading Room. The last time I offered him cookies with his coffee, he glanced at the packaging then scolded me for buying biscuits with a high fat content. Apparently, Goddess helped him lose twenty-four pounds. Lately, he only ever talks about Goddess and whether they should buy a house in or outside of town. Sometimes I feel a tinge of nostalgia when I think about those afternoons over coffee and cookies. We're still in touch regularly. He came with me when I bought my new car. I was surprised how civil he was with the salesman. He even gave me a housewarming gift. It's the book *House Repairs for Dummies.*

Edith is so busy in her role as Interim Head of Special Collections, she's lost interest in telling me what I should be doing. I went by her office one day, a first for me. She didn't have time to chat. "I'm busy as an eavesdropper with a party line," she said. Mercedes has stopped trying to fix me up with nurses or any women. I've been officially discharged as her patient. She's more concerned about the health of my house than about me. Cyril is gradually recovering from the disappointment of not having another man on his premises. Two or three times a week, after supper on a fine evening, he drives out for a visit. We sit on the veranda with Folio at my feet, alert to any move, sound or smell. We talk about the price of clapboard, the best quality of paints, about how soon I'll need to have the roof tarred again or about the state of the cod fishery.

Apart from that, not much else has changed. I still can't swim except with a life jacket, still know nothing as far as Henry is concerned, still sound like a foreigner and still have two small beach rocks in my pocket. It's natural for some things to stay the same. Take for example the retriever's instinct to retrieve, the view of the horizon from the top of a cliff on a day without fog, the taste of salt and smoke on skin after a bonfire in a cove, the tenderness of the hand that consoles or the unthinkable terror before the nightmare's climax. It's also natural for some things to change. Eventually, the ripple collapses on the surface of the pond, high tide becomes low, miscalculations evolve into opportunities, the fool becomes wiser.

Henry calls in the distance. "Back off with the *Chicken Bouillon Cube for the Soul*. Make your point!"

My point is that not much has changed. Not even in spite of the lessons. I could practice forever with swimming and still drown without the life jacket. No amount of lessons will make me pass for a Newfoundlander. I never was clever at lessons. It's about time I admitted it. Of course, I was a star at mathematics. My teachers used to say my ability had flooded into one area and parched the others in consequence. They didn't know about my talent for memorizing. A *Fahrenheit 451* scenario is unlikely but it's always best to be prepared. I know *Robinson Crusoe* by heart now. It's convenient to be able to draw on any page or section of the story no matter where or when. I have a collection of favourite passages, including this one:

> *I had now brought my state of life to be much easier in itself than it was at first, and much easier to my mind, as well as to my body…I learned to look more upon the bright side of my condition, and less upon the dark side, and to consider what I enjoyed rather than what I wanted.*

It's the type of ending I would have predicted for Crusoe's tale. As far as my own tale goes, it doesn't have a *happily-ever-after* sort of ending. It's more of a *once-upon-a-time* ending. Henry would probably say, "It was a long-time-coming ending. Give me the abridged version next time."

ACKNOWLEDGEMENTS

Thanks to the Writers' Alliance of Newfoundland and Labrador for its support. I'm grateful for the Writer-in-Residence program at Memorial University, Newfoundland and Labrador, which gave me the opportunity to receive feedback from some of the finest minds in Canada: Don McKay and Michael Crummey. Mark Callanan is another of those brilliant minds. I could not have wished for a better editor. At Breakwater Books, thank you to Annamarie Beckel for the encouragement I needed to see this book to the end and to Rebecca Rose and Rhonda Molloy as well. Thank you to the expert eyes of librarians Anne Hart, Lorraine Jackson and Suzanne Sexty.

Thanks to the following friends and family who read and commented: Dianne Anderson, Jack Eastwood, Louis Fortier, my son Adrian Gagnon, Carolyn Morgan, the Murphy crowd (Barbara, Anne, Paula [Lewis], Janet [MacDuff], Kieran), Marie Wadden and Elizabeth Yeoman.

I would like to acknowledge three sources I relied on to write the novel. These are: *A Gentle Madness: Bibliophiles, Bibliomanes, and the Eternal Passion for Books* by Nicholas A. Basbanes, "The Library of Babel" by Jorge Luis Borges, and the *Library at Night* by Alberto Manguel.